THE
BRIDGE

FINAL KINGDOM BOOK THREE

STEVEN K. SMITH

MD3 PRESS

Editing by: Kim Sheard (anotherviewediting.com)

Proofreading by: Stephanie Parent (polgarusstudio.com)

Book Cover Design by www.ebooklaunch.com

For more information, contact us at:

MyBoys3 Press, P.O. Box 2555, Midlothian, VA 23113

www.myboys3.com

First Printing

ISBN: 978-1-947881-14-3

To Mr. Lightcap and Mr. McKay,
for making 7th and 10th grade English memorable

THE
BRIDGE

The first rays of the early morning sun glistened off the polished stainless steel and glass of the futuristic desk. Like everything else in the gleaming office tower that rose high above the massive skyline, it was high-tech and space-age, constructed from the same materials used in fighter jets and machines of war. While many of the world's titans of industry fashioned their offices in dark wood grain and aged mahogany steeped in generations of wealth, Yao preferred to surround himself with visions of innovation, not tired vestiges of days gone by.

It was his morning ritual to sit on the floor of his office, spine forced straight, knees just centimeters from the wall of glass. The sun inched over the horizon, illuminating the city below him. His daily meditation ritual drew his mind above the petty needs of the masses that surrounded him in the city below, much of which was under his control. Even as he approached his eightieth year of life, Yao strove to keep his mind clear and sharp despite his body's rapid deterioration.

A soft knock sounded at the door, breaking his concentration. Yao released one last long exhale. His breath flowed in its distinctive but customary clucking sound, a result of a botched throat surgery several years past. He grasped his cane, artfully carved from a bamboo pole, and then rose gingerly to his feet, his joints crackling and popping in protest. His lips tightened into a thin, straight line as he moved to his desk.

"Enter," Yao responded confidently with a hint of annoyance.

A middle-aged man cracked the door open for a glance and then approached the desk. Johannes Sturgis, Ph.D., had been amongst his inner circle for years. While every other worker in his Shanghai headquarters was a fellow countryman, the tall Swede had long held Yao's trust. Sturgis had been handpicked by Yao from Stockholm University nearly two decades ago, and he knew more than anyone how ferociously Yao managed his routine. To risk the consequence of such an interruption, it must be something important.

"My apologies, sir," Sturgis said. "But this could not wait."

"What is it?"

Sturgis held out an electronic tablet and motioned to the chair in front of the desk. "May I?"

Yao nodded faintly, and Sturgis pulled the chair closer. "Our tracking has seen some movement, I'm afraid."

"Movement? When?"

"Largely in the past twenty-four hours." Sturgis pulled up a colorful image on his tablet that showed deep clusters of green and purple scattered across a grid.

It reminded Yao of the nuclear PET scans the doctors used to track the aggressive tumors that were secretly ravaging his body.

"This is two weeks ago." Sturgis adjusted the time lapse on the image and pointed at the colors. "And this is yesterday." In the more recent image, the greens had grouped into dense patterns, like when tracking a building thunderstorm on radar. "The cosmic abnormalities are deepening and growing in their consistency since the bridge was closed."

Yao studied the colors across the screen intently, as if he were deciphering some ancient language. "And your level of confidence?"

Sturgis cleared his throat. "We were skeptical at first, as you know, but these developments are quite conclusive. A fissure has clearly formed between the dimensional realms, most likely produced by the last quantum transmissions."

Yao finally looked away from the screen. He leaned back into his chair, shaping his thin fingers into a triangle as he stared at the wall over Sturgis's shoulder.

The other man shifted uncomfortably in his seat as he waited for a more complete reaction. "We now believe the situation could become much more grim than we'd anticipated."

"We'll cross that bridge when we come to it."

Sturgis shifted again in his chair. "That's what we're afraid of, sir. Mr. Fitz believes it is only a matter of time until the reactions chip away at the cosmic infrastructure. It could permanently reopen the bridge between the dimensions."

Yao clucked his tongue at the mention of Fitz. Despite his programming genius, the fat man created more messes than he was worth. "His location and messages remain secure?"

Sturgis nodded. "They are as they should be, aside from his constant grousing over being dispatched to Northern Alberta. Despite his girth, the man doesn't seem to enjoy the cold. I told him it reminds me of Stockholm, but he won't hear it."

Yao shook his head. "Mr. Fitz's comfort is not my concern. He'd do well to remember the potential fallout of any discovery of his communications or his location and keep his messages to required information only." Yao paused briefly, then added, "And the other?"

Sturgis pushed his chair back and stood. "I'm afraid Ms. Avanair has not reported for her last two check-ins. Her situation seems to be considerably more challenging. She is, as they say, 'in the wind.'"

Yao nodded and waved his hand dismissively. "Very well. Keep me posted, Mr. Sturgis."

"Yes, sir." The man made a slight bow and then exited the room.

Yao swiveled his chair to face the window. The sun had climbed higher, now reflecting brightly against the neighboring skyscrapers. While he had often dreamt of a day when the Red Dragon of China would rise up to dominate the loathsome nations and culture of the Western world, he was no longer consumed with his nation's future. His singular focus was now on maintaining his personal dominance before he breathed his last, even if it required using unorthodox methods. As his physical body neared its natural expiration date, he would leverage this new technology to carry him into a new existence within the virtual world.

He considered Sturgis's update. It was certainly not the news he'd desired. As a young man, Yao had despised surprises. He'd manipulated his world to avoid the unexpected at all costs. But as the years went by, he'd discovered the truth: that life is a series of adjustments. He'd learned to embrace the unexpected, nimbly adapting to each new volley fired at him. Even so, he yearned for his future life in the virtual world, where he had designed an existence of pure mastery and dominance.

The quantum machines that he and his competitors had developed were pushing the limits of science, and not even he was so bold as to predict what consequences may result from a tear in the cosmic fabric. Still, his inner narcissist was intrigued by the news. Yao wasn't above leaving a wake of earthly destruction in his wake as he hastily rocketed across dimensions to his new kingdom.

His one regret was not stamping out his competition—the JOSHUA project, headed by William Hendrickson and his loose connection to the American government. Yao had lured Mr. Fitz from his position working with Hendrickson and their government contracts years ago, feeding into the man's inflated ego. It had been Fitz's vision to build Q2 as a gaming division. They'd developed *Final Kingdom* as a Trojan horse of sorts to identify and herd top programming minds to their stables. Neither of them had dreamed that the game would quickly achieve such worldwide popularity, but it had excellently served its purpose while significantly padding their research coffers.

Bryce Pearson had been one of many who'd been recruited through the game; however, he was also the reason Yao's team had been forced into hiding all over the globe. The young man had proven to be quite resourceful, both when working with Q2 and against them. In a surprising act of courage and ingenuity, he'd fled across the digital bridge. He still ran free within the virtual world despite pursuit from Rangers and attacks against his younger brother and family in the real world.

Bryce had also released a virus into Eden's mainframe that, combined with the attention drawn by the opening of the bridge, had required the abandonment of Q2's mountain compound. Sturgis had been able to quickly retreat from their scientific compound in America and join Yao in the safety and anonymity of the Chinese mainland. Fitz, however, had been too slow and had to be jettisoned through back-channel arrangements across the Canadian border. In addition, the beautiful Heather Avanair, lead handler and programming team administrator, had gone underground. Only a handful of her scattered communications had made their way back to Yao's people in the weeks since the incident. But she was a dedicated member of the team and well trained in keeping silent on the proprietary nature of their efforts. That said, he'd have preferred her to be in-house.

Yao would allow young Bryce to hide for now, but it was only a matter of time until his former recruit met his inevitable demise.

CHAPTER TWO

Z ach blinked, making sure his mind wasn't deceiving him. But there it was again. Staring at him from the other side of the river was the same fox that had led him to Bryce's video message in the canyon cave inside *Kingdom*. The same fox he'd seen in the field that separated his house from Maggie and Jess's neighborhood.

"Do you think it's him?" Andrew whispered, his voice barely audible.

"I don't know," Zach replied slowly. It was the same fox, but was it Bryce?

"It could be a trap," said Jess, angling her head as if she could see around the bushes, even though the riverbank was inside the digital world of *Kingdom* and was displayed on the wall monitor in Zach's room. But after everything they'd been through, he didn't blame her. The line between the virtual world and the real one had become thin. Danger-ously thin.

Zach self-consciously reached up and touched the patch of hair just above his ear. He could almost still feel the sensation of warping across dimensions, from when Ji Yao had forced him into the JOSHUA machine back at the cavern. He often relived the feeling of plunging into the deep pool inside *Kingdom*. Of seeing Bryce, face-to-face.

But it had ended too suddenly. It was all wrong. After Dr. Hendrickson and Tyler Barnes had activated the machine with the code on Maggie's necklace, Bryce had guided Zach through *Kingdom's* levels to a return portal at the chasm. But as the bridge opened, and the brilliant green stream of light poured from the clouds to bring them home, Bryce had been pulled back. The Sportsman, a fierce virtual Ranger, had snagged Bryce in his fishing line. The lasting image in Zach's mind was of his older brother's face, broken in resignation as Zach plummeted away from him across the bridge and back to the real world.

They'd been so close to bringing Bryce home, but now he was worlds away, and the bridge was closed. Every day after school, Andrew, Jess, and Zach had methodically mapped out each quadrant within the game, level by level, desperately seeking where the Rangers may have taken Bryce. They'd recorded each session. Sometimes Zach even went back and re-watched their rounds at night, searching for anything they could have missed. But there had been nothing—until now.

As the green-eyed fox blinked back at them on the screen, a trace of hope filled Zach's heart for the first time in weeks. Maybe there still was a chance. Maybe Bryce could still get home.

A crash sounded from the field east of the river. A squadron of Rangers burst through the brush, their heavy weaponry at the ready.

"Watch out!" shrieked Jess, quickly activating her defense mode and diving into a shadowy overhang carved into the side of the riverbank.

"Where did they come from?" said Andrew, his avatar following her into hiding. He elbowed Zach in real life. "Dude, take cover!"

Zach hesitated for a moment, glancing back to look for the fox. But it had disappeared. Had it really been Bryce, or was Zach's imagination running wild again? There was no time to think about it. He maneuvered his controller so that his avatar hid with the others in the cutout's safety. Three heavily armed Rangers stomped over the rocks and onto the soft ground beside the river.

Zach eyed the middle Ranger carefully.

"Is that the Sportsman?" whispered Andrew.

Zach nodded and then whispered, "I think so," as if anything they said in his bedroom could be heard through *Kingdom's* game interface. That seemed impossible, but again, the line had blurred so much that he honestly wasn't sure anymore.

They lay frozen for a full minute until the avatars of the gunmen had fully left the screen. Zach was afraid to hit the pause button, but he finally did and glanced at his friends. "That was Bryce, right?"

"It seemed like the fox was looking at us," said Jess.

"Do you think he's gone?" asked Andrew.

"Probably, with those Rangers around," Zach answered. "But that means he's okay."

"Or at least as okay as he can be trapped inside *Kingdom*," said Andrew.

Jess pulled off her headset and stood. "Let's get Maggie. We need to go talk with my brother."

CHAPTER THREE

Zach glanced at Andrew and Jess in the backseat. The last time they'd driven to Tech, the Sportsman had sliced and diced Maggie's Jeep along the curvy mountain roads leading from Dr. Hendrickson's mountain cabin. That was three months ago, but it felt like yesterday. The only difference now was that Maggie was driving her dad's hand-me-down Ford Explorer. They hadn't known how to explain the damage to the Jeep, but the story she'd made up for her parents of being attacked by a deranged, rabid elk was hard for even Zach to believe.

"You sure Tyler will be here?" Andrew asked as Maggie pulled into the parking lot closest to Lightcap Hall, Tech's main science and technology building.

"He said he could meet with us," Jess replied. Her relationship with her older brother had started fading away when he'd begun working for Hendrickson as a graduate student and had basically disappeared from her life. But when Jess, Zach, Andrew, and Maggie had parachuted into the middle of the top-secret JOSHUA project, Jess and Tyler had suddenly been thrust back together.

"What about Hendrickson?" Maggie asked.

"Tyler said he's tied up in a meeting," said Jess. "Some kind of review with the military bigwigs from Washington."

"Military?" said Andrew, raising his eyebrows. "What do they want?"

Jess sighed. "Relax, will you? It's some kind of standard review. A lot of Hendrickson's funding comes from the government, remember?"

"Yeah, I remember," said Andrew. "But knowing that and relaxing are two different things. I don't want them dropping a nuke in the middle of Milton."

"Why would they do that?" asked Zach.

Andrew shrugged. "Who knows, but nothing about this stuff makes me relaxed."

Zach knew what he meant. Andrew was his best friend, and while he often had a knack for the dramatic, for once he might not be overreacting. The world had seemed like it was coming apart at the seams ever since they'd discovered the truth behind Bryce's disappearance. Learning that high-tech quantum propulsion machines could cross into alternate dimensions was enough to make anyone jumpy. Since his return to the real world, Zach had started seeing ghosts in every shadow. There was no telling what hidden secrets existed around him, waiting to challenge all he knew to be true.

They took the elevator up to the fourth floor of

Lightcap Hall. The halls were mostly empty on a Saturday. Tyler met them in the hallway on the way to Hendrickson's office.

"Hey, guys." He looked tense.

"Thanks for meeting with us," Maggie said.

"Something wrong?" asked Jess.

"Big meeting in the lecture hall," Tyler replied. "General Weber's in from DC. He's been meeting with Hendrickson all morning."

"I knew it." Andrew placed his palm over his forehead. "They're gonna nuke us all."

Tyler lowered his eyebrows. "What?"

Jess shot Andrew a glare as she tugged on Tyler's elbow. "Just ignore him. We have a lot to tell you."

As they walked toward Hendrickson's office, two double doors across the hall opened and a bustle of activity streamed out of the room. Once the first wave of people had exited, Zach could see half a dozen men dressed in formal military uniforms stood around the first two rows of seats, closing laptops and gathering papers into folders and briefcases. Several of the men had long rows of medals and impressive-looking stars and insignias pinned to their jackets. Tyler motioned the four of them to the far side of the hallway as the military men filed out.

Zach saw Professor Hendrickson near the front of the room. He was in a conversation with a stern-looking officer with a gray buzz cut and an extra-long collection of pins on his uniform. It wasn't much of a conversation, actually. Hendrickson was just nodding at the man's rapid-fire speech like he was a quarterback being chewed out by a football coach.

"Is that General Weber?" whispered Maggie.

Tyler nodded.

"He looks tough," muttered Andrew. "But I bet I could take him."

"Let's just say he doesn't suffer fools gladly," replied Tyler, stepping further out of the way as the two men entered the hallway.

Jess nudged Andrew in the ribs. "Just stay away from him." Andrew was about to argue back, but Tyler shook his head.

As the general and Professor Hendrickson walked past, the formidable-looking military man paused and stared at the group of kids against the wall. It seemed to Zach like the general was glaring right at him. The imposing stare finally moved on when the general turned and said something to the professor as they waited for the elevator, but Zach couldn't hear what it was. Were they working on bringing Bryce home? Did the general know that Zach was his brother?

When the last of the officials had left and the elevator doors closed, Dr. Hendrickson sighed dramatically. He walked back to the group waiting in the hall. He looked exhausted.

"How'd it go?" Tyler asked tentatively.

"About as you'd imagine," Dr. Hendrickson answered. "A million expectations, with not enough funding and too little time." He turned and nodded at the rest of them waiting along the wall. "What are you kids doing here today? Did we have an appointment?"

"No," Zach replied. "But we have to talk to you. Something happened."

A pained expression flooded the professor's face. "Of course it did." He rubbed the back of his neck. "Why don't you have a seat in the conference room and I'll be with you in a few minutes. I think I need another cup of coffee."

"Thanks," Maggie said.

Tyler led them into the conference room, and they all sat around the long table. It felt odd to know that a military general and his team had just been sitting in the same space.

"Is it good news or bad?" Tyler asked.

"Um…" said Zach, looking around the table. "It's hard to say."

When Dr. Hendrickson entered a couple minutes later, he sat at the head of the table with an oversized coffee and a notepad. He took a short sip and then looked up at them. "Okay, that should help. So what's going on?"

"We saw Bryce," Zach blurted. There was no point beating around the bush.

Hendrickson glanced at Tyler with a flash of surprise, but then he turned back to Zach. "You saw him? Saw him where?"

"In the game. Inside *Kingdom*."

"It wasn't his physical body," said Jess. "It was the fox again."

"So it was the avatar he'd used in the past to communicate with you," said Tyler.

"Right," Zach answered, and then detailed more of the scene at the river.

"And you're sure it was the same fox?" Tyler said as he typed notes into his laptop.

"It was him," Zach said confidently. There was no question in his mind. "It had the same green eyes."

"Did you speak to him?" Dr. Hendrickson asked.

"No. A squad of Rangers stormed over the bank and we had to hide," said Andrew.

"When we looked up, he was gone," said Zach.

Maggie leaned forward in her chair. "But that means he's okay, right? If the Rangers still had him, he wouldn't have been able to use the fox to signal us."

"Possibly," said Hendrickson, pausing for a long drink of his coffee.

"Possibly?" Zach's voice rose. "We can't just leave him in there. Now we know he's safe, or at least free from the Rangers. We have to do something. He's reaching out to us!"

Dr. Hendrickson nodded and held up his hand. "I understand, Zach, but I'm afraid it's not that simple."

"What do you mean?" asked Jess.

Dr. Hendrickson sighed and took another drink. "Things have gotten... complicated."

Zach felt his insides turn. "Complicated?"

"What do you mean?" said Maggie.

Dr. Hendrickson tried a smile. "That was General Weber I just met with. He's the military liaison for the joint chiefs at the Pentagon. He's briefed them on everything that's happened with JOSHUA and Q2. The general's taken a keen interest in our operations, the implications of what our technology can do, and the impact of crossing into the virtual dimension. Most importantly, they're concerned about Yao and what he might be working on from China."

He paused like he was considering what more to say and then looked straight at Zach. "The general is also suspicious that Bryce might still be under Q2's control, despite everything that's happened."

"You have to be kidding," said Maggie.

"They think Bryce is still working for Yao?" exclaimed Zach.

"We're not saying that's true," explained Tyler. "But the military takes these things very seriously."

Zach's face was hot. "Yeah, well, I take it seriously too. And I'm telling you, Bryce is not working for them. Those monsters tried to kill him. They tried to kill all of us! And in case you forgot, I was inside *Kingdom* too. Maybe they should ask *me* what's going on. I'll be happy to give them—"

The professor held up his hand, his expression serious. "That's not going to happen, Zach. I'll remind you that we discussed this at length previously. You're not to tell anyone outside this room about crossing the bridge. I assure you, it's for your own good."

Zach rolled his eyes and leaned back in his chair. Hendrickson was convinced that if the government or people like General Weber knew he'd been in the virtual world, they'd lock him up and subject him to a litany of interrogations and tests. He'd reluctantly agreed not to say anything, knowing it would crush his mom and dad to have another son disappear, but he wasn't happy about it. Zach knew Hendrickson was trying to look out for his welfare, but it was annoying. While he wished he could share with the general what he'd seen and done, the last thing he wanted was to be poked and prodded by a bunch of doctors and scientists. Hendrickson was right about that part. Zach couldn't help Bryce get home if he was locked up in some quarantine bubble.

"It's just… maybe if the general knew what I'd done, what I'd seen happen, he might take Bryce's situation more seriously."

Tyler gave Jess a look. She put a hand on Zach's shoulder from the next seat. "That's too dangerous, Zach."

"But what about Bryce?" said Maggie.

"I promise you both, we're working on it." Professor Hendrickson's tone was softer. "No one has forgotten about Bryce." When he glanced back at Zach, it seemed like he was staring at the place where the white patch had appeared in Zach's hair. "Are you still feeling okay?"

Zach touched the spot self-consciously. The streak had first appeared after a strange electrical current had zapped his hand in the field where he'd seen the fox. When he came back across the bridge from inside *Kingdom*, it had grown, covering nearly the whole right side of his head. In order to hide the truth from his parents, Maggie had helped him cover it up with some hair dye she'd gotten from a friend whose mom worked in a salon.

The reality was that Zach still felt occasional tremors. They reminded him of the shock he'd received in the field behind his house, when he'd blacked out and woken up flat on his back with the Harpers' dog licking him in the face. But he hadn't told anyone else they were happening.

"I'm fine," he lied. "But I'm not who you need to be worrying about. It's Bryce that needs you, and I feel like everyone's just giving up on him."

Hendrickson's lips narrowed. "I'm not giving up. It's just taking longer than I'd like. Some things have moved outside my control." His phone buzzed on the table. He glanced at it and then stood. "I'm afraid I need to go. I realize this is frustrating for you, but try to have patience." He smiled weakly and then strode into the hall, speaking into his phone as he left.

Jess looked across the table at her brother. "Can't you do something?"

Tyler bounced his head back and forth. "Believe me, we're trying, Jess. But like he said, things have gotten complicated. There are other things going on."

"Other things?" asked Andrew.

Tyler glanced at the clock on the wall. "Have you eaten?"

"Not yet," said Maggie.

Tyler pushed his chair back. "How about some lunch? We can talk more there." He walked around the table toward the doorway, resting his hand on Zach's shoulder when he passed. "Okay?"

"Sure," Zach muttered.

CHAPTER FOUR

They all settled into the corner booth in the sandwich shop a few blocks from campus, having picked out their lunches at the counter. Zach watched Tyler unwrap his ham and Swiss methodically, folding each corner of the paper into squares.

Jess shook her head. "Don't ask, it's a weird thing he does."

Maggie eyed Tyler suspiciously. "Is there something you're not telling us?"

Tyler glanced around to make sure no one was within earshot. "There's more happening than you know. Or at least we think there is."

"Will you just spill it, Ty," said Jess. "We don't have time for all this cloak and dagger crap."

"Listen," said Tyler. "It's not that simple. Like the professor said, the military has really limited what we can do. While we used to have free rein when we were developing JOSHUA, now they're watching everything, asking a million questions, and then asking them again before letting us do the smallest thing."

Zach rested his elbows on the table and stared at him. "Bryce is counting on us."

"I know that. And it's the only reason we're talking right now." He scanned the room again as if there were spies lurking at the soda fountain machine. "You can't speak a word of this to anyone."

"Uh, I think we know that by now, dude," said Andrew.

"Ty," moaned Jess, "quit stalling."

Tyler nodded and looked at Zach. "Ever since you came back across the bridge, we've been getting some unusual readings."

"What kind of readings?" asked Maggie.

"We're not entirely sure, but there are now some abnormalities in the atmosphere's magnetic field that we've never seen before. Imagine small traces of radiation on a Geiger counter, but different." Tyler took a bite of his sandwich.

"That doesn't sound good," said Jess.

Andrew shook his head. "I'll bet Yao is testing his nuclear arsenal in the South China Sea right now. It's always nukes."

Zach elbowed him in the ribs. "Shut up." He turned back to Tyler. "So what does that mean? Did something happen when we crossed?"

"Maybe. We don't know yet, which is part of what worries us. It's like when a previously unknown virus starts spreading. It might be mostly harmless, but until we identify a way to test it and develop treatments or a vaccine, everyone will remain wary. Right now, the general is the one who is wary of anything to do with bridging these worlds."

"So General Weber knows about the readings?" asked Jess.

Tyler nodded. "Like I said, we have to tell them everything now." He nodded at Zach solemnly. "Or at least most things."

"So what does that mean for Bryce?" asked Maggie.

Zach stared at his food but suddenly didn't feel hungry. "It shouldn't change anything. He's still there, and we have to find a way to open the bridge to get him home. After that, I don't care what they do with any of it. I'd be happy if I never heard about *Final Kingdom* ever again."

"I know," said Tyler. "And the professor's being straight with you when he says we're working on it. I met Bryce, remember? I keep picturing him how he was in the dark parking lot on the side of the mountain. They scared him enough to get him to feed me code from Eden. That took a lot of courage, and it was the only way we could get the JOSHUA machine operational fast enough to combat Yao and his team. I know what he's going through, and I want him back home. Maybe not to the same extreme that you do, but it's important to me that we help him. I could have just as easily have been the one trapped in *Kingdom*."

Jess raised her eyebrows. "What do you mean?"

Tyler sipped his drink. "The original plan was for me to test the JOSHUA machine. I was going to be the first person to cross the bridge into the virtual world. But then

Q2's Eden machine jumped ahead of us with their flurry of new programming recruits like Bryce. Everything was turned on its head when Bryce went across, and then again when Yao sent you."

Zach felt everyone's eyes turn to him just as Tyler's phone buzzed. He glanced at it. "That's Hendrickson. He needs me back in his office. I've gotta go." He took a big bite before carefully wrapping up the rest of his sandwich.

"Everything all right?" asked Jess.

"None of this is all right," Tyler replied. "But I promise I'll get back to you as soon as I have more information. And remember what I said. This stays with us. Not a word to anyone, or I'll be sitting with you on the outside and won't be able to help Bryce either. Understood?"

"Yeah," muttered Zach. "We got it."

Andrew shook his head as Tyler left the table. "This is messed up."

"They're trying," said Jess. "Ty's right, I'm sure it's a lot harder with the military breathing down their necks."

Andrew glanced out the window. "Looks like he changed his mind."

"Who?" Zach asked.

"Tyler." Andrew pointed to the entrance. "He's coming back."

They all looked up as Tyler neared their table. His face looked serious.

"What's wrong?" asked Jess.

"There's been a development," Tyler replied, sliding back onto the bench.

"Already?" asked Andrew.

Tyler nodded. "The FBI detained someone from Q2 this morning. They're bringing them in right now. General Weber has ordered that everyone involved in the situation must report for further questioning. That includes all of us."

"The FBI!" Andrew exclaimed.

"Who is it?" Zach asked, his mind spinning. "Who did they capture?"

Tyler shook his head. "They didn't say. But it sounds like someone important." He stood from the table. "We need to go. They're sending a transport for us now. You can call your parents on the way."

CHAPTER FIVE

The flashlight had seemed dim since he'd dropped it on the rock, but it could also have been Bryce's imagination. Electronic devices didn't seem to work the same way in *Kingdom*'s virtual world, but regardless, it was harder to see than it had been. Maybe a fog was rolling in, turning the air thick and harder to penetrate.

Bryce marched on, tirelessly following the curve of the river across fields, through wooded forests, and over the ever-changing terrains of multiple levels within *Kingdom*. He was exhausted, but he knew he couldn't stop moving. He could never stop. Not if he wanted to get home.

The Rangers were still out there, tracking him, pursuing him like prey, but his energy was fading faster than his flashlight beam, and he needed at least a little rest. He'd put a good distance between them by now. It might be enough to get a couple hours of sleep.

One of the many perils of running from avatars like the

Rangers was that they didn't require rest. They just kept going. They'd catch him, eventually; it was only a matter of time. But he had to drag things out as long as possible, if only to give the others back home more time.

Bryce didn't know why the bridge remained closed. Tyler and Hendrickson must be working hard to get one of the transport machines operational. They had to be. He refused to spend the rest of his days in this virtual world, although if the Rangers found him, there might not be many days left to worry about.

He'd been so close to getting home. When he'd jumped off the ring of stones surrounding the chasm portal, he could almost see Milton, his parents, and Maggie. But then he felt the tug of the Sportsman's fishing line on his ankle. It had yanked him back into the virtual world like a deadly rip current dragging him out to sea. He'd let go of Zach's hand and watched his little brother vanish into the swirling green glow.

It was the only choice. As much as Bryce longed to get home, he'd never intended to involve Zach, let alone send him spiraling into the virtual world. Not only had Bryce brought this all on himself, he'd put his loved ones in peril. And if that weren't bad enough, Charlie and Rachel were dead. It was crushing.

After Zach fell through the portal, the Sportsman had reeled Bryce up the chasm's rocky edge like an angler landing a trophy fish. Bryce had felt his life slipping away with each pull of the line. The real world and all he'd loved had been right in front of him, but was now so very far away.

But then came an unexpected turn. Just as the Sportsman pulled Bryce from the chasm, his face stretched in a devilish grin, one of the night cats pounced from the tree line. It knocked the tall Ranger off balance just enough to dislodge the fishing rod from his hands. Bryce had been thrown forward and had instinctively reached for a rocky crevice in the chasm wall. While the Ranger was distracted by the onslaught of still more creatures, Bryce had inched his way up to the mouth of the chasm. He'd climbed over the ring of stones and then sprinted across the clearing to the cover of the forest. By the time the Sportsman had extricated himself from the attacking cats, Bryce was a half mile into the trees. He'd been running ever since.

But now he could not run any longer. If he didn't stop to rest, he would collapse—he could feel it. He moved further from the river trail, spying a dense thicket that might have once served as an animal den, a fox's perhaps. He shined his light at the base of the surrounding bushes, finally glimpsing an opening just large enough for him to slide through. No creature, fox or otherwise, looked to be occupying the space. It should keep him hidden and protected for a couple hours of sleep.

Kingdom's virtual world did strange things to his body. On one hand, he didn't need to eat, drink, sleep, or relieve himself in the same ways as back home, but occasionally he would drink from a spring or eat a cluster of grapes or berries. While it may not have been critical for survival, the treats were even more delicious than back home and provided short boosts of energy, like a sugar rush. Sleep was similar, but every day here was grueling and there was little else to do at night. His endless flight from the Rangers was exhausting, and a couple hours of rest kept him refreshed.

Bryce squeezed into the thicket, avoiding all but a few thorns. He collapsed flat on the ground with only his pack to support his head. He lay still, listening for signs of trouble, but he heard only the ripple of water from the river and a gentle breeze rustling leaves in the trees. With his eyes closed, he was transported back to camping trips along the Snake River with Dad and Zach, to campfires, marshmallows and smores, and telling stories.

He forced his eyes open. It still hurt too much to dwell on those thoughts. He stared up at the stiff, sharp thorns. A growing part of him believed he would spend whatever days remained wandering alone through this desolate, artificial world that had become his home.

He peered through a gap in the thicket at the night sky. After all this time, it was one of the few things that still threw him. Each evening, the dual suns dove for the horizon in just minutes, plunging the land into sudden darkness. The whiplash was worth it, though, for with the darkness came the most extraordinary nightscapes. He and Zach had discussed it on the lone evening they had spent together.

Bryce marveled at the wild formations of greens, blues, and oranges floating against the ebony background, like the nebulas he'd learned about in middle school science class.

The colors formed themselves into shapes as he looked, like puffy clouds over skies of blue. He saw a dragon, complete with a long, pointed tail and wide wings. At home, the shapes you saw in clouds were just your mind filling in the gaps—like a psychiatrist's inkblot test, you saw what your mind told you to see. Bryce knew that all this was just the results of the keystrokes of some innovative programmer somewhere in Q2's gaming division, yet lying beneath this sky was nothing short of magical. Maybe that's what magic really was—someone's intricate programming sequence designed to fool the senses.

His gaze followed the slope of the dragon's wide wings, and for an instant, he could have sworn that they flapped. Did they move? That was more than he'd seen from any virtual programming. He stared back, catching another split-second of motion. It wasn't a flap, it was more like a shimmer—a glitch.

Hoping to see something that could help him to make sense of the shimmer, he stared further to the west and noticed a patch of sky that looked entirely out of place. It was completely devoid of stars, and its dull gray was a different shade from the rest of the night's deep black, like it was a portion of the canvas that a master painter had forgotten to fill. In all his countless nights in *Kingdom*, he'd never seen this before. He stared at the sky for a long time, but eventually his eyelids grew heavy, exhaustion overtook his body, and he drifted off.

CHAPTER SIX

B ryce jerked awake, his head rising into a painful tangle of sharp thorns. For a moment, he'd forgotten where he was, but his flight from the Rangers quickly flooded back. Something had woken him. Had it just been a dream? The forest was eerily quiet in the faint morning light. He felt, more than heard, the noise of marching footsteps coming down a hill. Adrenaline surged through his body.

The Rangers were coming. He had to move. Now.

Bryce slid from his hiding place, pulled on his pack, and bolted through the forest. He leapt over branches and trees, searching desperately for the river trail. But there was no time. Shouts came from behind him as the squadron locked onto his position like a bloodhound on the scent.

The sharp clip of gunfire pierced the still air. Bryce broke to the right just in time, diving forward as a tree trunk splintered apart inches from his head. He darted in and out of the trees, the voices still behind him but dropping further back. There was occasional gunfire, but nothing landed close to him.

A clearing appeared up ahead. The open space would make his running easier, but at the same time, provide a clear target for the attackers. There was no other option. He couldn't turn back toward the Rangers, so he continued on at breakneck speed.

As he reached the tree line at the edge of the clearing, he leapt over a collection of vines. While he was in midair, a searing pain ripped across his right leg. He landed in the clearing, grasping at his leg, his hands now red with blood. Had they shot him? He hadn't heard gunfire.

He looked back and saw a strand of barbed wire hidden amongst the vines. Its menacing metal razors had ripped straight through his pants and gashed his leg. Bryce knew he had to keep moving. He gritted his teeth and forced himself to his feet. He hobbled into the field as a burning pain surged through his body.

He wouldn't be able to continue for long. The wound needed pressure to stop the bleeding. Another shot was fired behind him, wide and off target, but they'd narrow their aim soon enough. He was a sitting duck out in that field. He peered ahead and saw the river a hundred yards ahead. Again, he ignored the pain and moved faster. He zigzagged through the grass toward the river.

Glancing over his shoulder, Bryce saw the Rangers emerge from the forest. There were half a dozen, maybe more, all armed and dangerous.

The water was growing closer. He could hear it now, a fast-moving section of rapids. Fifty yards. Forty. He might make it.

Another shot rang out, nicking the edge of his pack. He ducked down and tumbled forward, but rolled quickly back to his feet and into a run. He pictured a sprint to the finish line in a track meet and willed his body forward.

Twenty yards. Ten. The grass was taller now, partially concealing him, but a good scope could still pick him off.

He glimpsed the riverbank and cut sharply to the water. There was no time to look back. He leapt over the edge and fell below the grass just as a rifle fired. A bullet screamed past his ear. He splashed into cool water. His leg burned like fire for an instant, but then the current caught him.

Bryce realized that this could be his escape. He sank his body low into the water, barely keeping his eyes and mouth above the surface. The river carried him faster than he could run. Would it be fast enough to elude the squadron of Rangers?

A bullet ricocheted off a rounded rock just ahead of him, but Bryce kept pushing with his arms, guiding his body through the rapids. He turned and saw the Rangers on the bank, guns pointed, but then the river took a sharp turn and they were out of sight.

He didn't have the time to worry about his leg. It was all he could do to keep balanced as he bobbed through the fast-moving water like a twig. The weight of his pack pulled him deeper in the water. He used his good leg to pinball away from the occasional rock that was poking up from the surface, but some he couldn't miss, and he banged his butt and lower back on those as he flew past them.

He looked up after one particularly hard bounce to see a giant rock dead ahead. It was as wide as Maggie's Jeep. A sharp edge jutted above the surface. He was headed straight for it.

Bryce strained to angle his movement away from the rock, but the pressure of the water made his arms feel tied down. The surging water had him in its grip. There was no navigating around it. He braced for impact, closing his eyes and gritting his teeth as he plowed into the rock.

But he didn't hit. When he opened his eyes, the view in front of him was clear. He wrenched his head around and saw the rock directly behind him, like he'd passed straight through. As he stared, dumbfounded, the rock flickered, like a screen with a bad monitor connection. How was that possible?

Bryce whipped back around to the view ahead of him. There was no more time to think about the rock. The water was racing faster in a descending elevation. He had no idea where the river led. It was like all of *Kingdom*'s levels, a mystery until the moment things suddenly changed.

The spray from the rapids was blinding. The water roared, moving faster and faster until it simply disappeared. One moment he was floating, the next he was falling, down, down, like the sudden drop in an amusement park ride.

Bryce soared over the waterfall, falling fifty feet to the bottom. Rocks would have splattered him on impact, but he plunged into a deep pool. He struggled to hold his breath, kicking with his good leg back toward the surface. His lungs burned like they had in the Eden machine when he'd crossed dimensions into the grain silo. But finally, just as his mind was turning dark, his head crested the surface and he gasped for air.

The current had subsided, but a torrential spray of water filled the air from the crashing waterfall. He breathed deeply, refreshing his lungs as his body floated gently toward the bank. When his feet felt the ground, he crawled forward. He collapsed in the soft dirt, exhausted. His right calf burned, and blood had stained his pants leg red. But he was alive.

Bryce raised his head. A thick forest surrounded the river. He wasn't sure how far the water had carried him, but it seemed to have rescued him from the Rangers. At least for now.

CHAPTER SEVEN

B ryce wandered into the forest, desperate for a place to rest. He spied a rocky outcropping at the base of an incline, nearly hidden from view behind the trees. The formations reminded him of the place he'd hidden Rachel after the Rangers shot her. Those mountains were far away now, but maybe it was a sign that this could be the protected place he needed. He crouched down and felt cool, moist air pouring from a small opening. As he climbed through, he discovered the space opened up to a much wider area.

He settled on a smooth rock, wincing at the constant pain. Most of the bleeding in his leg had been stopped by the water, but it still throbbed where the razor wire had gashed his calf. He squeezed the water from the last remaining cloth bandage in his pack and wrapped his leg tightly. He needed to be able to keep moving, and it would be nearly impossible to do so if he didn't take care of the wound now.

Bryce tried to pinpoint his position. The waterfall had been the start of a new level. He could easily feel it now, almost like he was developing a sense for this place. Was it becoming more open to him, or was he slowly becoming a part of it? What effects was it having on his body? He, Rachel, and Zach were the only humans to have ventured inside this virtual world. Rachel hadn't been inside long enough to develop any side effects. The white spot in Zach's hair seemed to have been caused by the interactions with the Ranger and the electricity he'd been touched by in the field. But that happened back home, not here inside *Kingdom.* Maybe that was the problem —interacting with virtual things in the real world. He hoped that the white streak of hair was all that had happened to Zach. But he hadn't seen his brother since he'd crossed back over the bridge. Who knew what side effects could have come from that.

Bryce pushed those thoughts from his mind. He couldn't go there. He had to stay positive about home and his possibility of getting there. If he allowed his mind to wander to those dark places, he'd never have the willpower to carry on.

He thought back to the rock in the river. It didn't make sense. He'd been just inches away, on a collision course, but there'd been no impact. It was like he'd momentarily disappeared and passed directly through the rock. Which was impossible. The rules may be different in a place like this, but he still should have smacked hard into the immovable stone, just like his clothes had become soaked from the water.

But he'd seen the rock flicker, just for a moment, like a glitch in a computer program or a computer screen with a loose connection. Maybe it was the rock that had disappeared. Or—he thought back to the night sky—it was something like the gray patch. Either way, something was happening in *Kingdom*.

As Bryce's mind reached that startling conclusion, his ears picked up a faint sound. It seemed to originate deeper within the cave. Had it been there all along, or had it just started? Maybe his ears had been waterlogged from his ride down the river. He listened closely to the low hum, which sounded like when the lights at the sports field turned on at dusk.

He switched on the flashlight from his pack. The beam was still dim, but it was holding on. The river apparently hadn't affected the flashlight, but power didn't seem to work the same in *Kingdom* as it did back home. The computer and communication devices in the hayloft at the country farm he'd found with Rachel had operated without wires or power outlets. Everything just seemed to work, as if the current was embedded in the atmosphere and the entire place was one giant electrical source.

Bryce stood and trained his light on the far wall, revealing a crevice that opened to a deeper tunnel. The cave seemed to fall lower, descending into—not the earth, but whatever you'd call the ground in this place.

Intrigued by the hum and the new cave, Bryce nearly

forgot about his leg as he squeezed through the opening. He followed the passage farther and farther, the faint beam of light bright enough to illuminate at least a few feet ahead of his steps. After a time, he realized he might never find his way back, but he sensed that he needed to reach whatever lay ahead.

A second sound gradually added to the humming. It was a slow, steady dripping of water. Formations of narrow pillars filled the surrounding space—stalagmites or stalactites, he couldn't remember which were which from earth science class. He was sure that the programmers who'd designed this tunnel must have patterned it from rock formations back on the literal Earth.

As the dripping grew louder, a stream emerged along the side of the tunnel. It gradually widened and flowed into the ground. He realized it must be a branch of the river he'd travelled on the surface. Soon, the passage leveled, and he stepped into a wide space holding a circular pool about the size of the one at the Milton YMCA. It was larger than the pool in the canyon where he'd found Zach. He shined his light into the water, but after the first couple feet from the ledge he was standing on, the bottom faded away and he couldn't guess its depth.

Bryce looked up at a high, smooth ceiling twenty feet above his head. There was no opening in the center like there had been above the canyon's pool. Logically, he knew he was far too deep within the ground for there to be a skylight, but the rock curved into a perfectly formed dome like it had been hand chiseled. The passage he'd been following seemed to reach a dead end at the pool, but without the sound of the dripping water, once again he could hear the electronic hum. Sound reverberated off the curved ceiling, bouncing off the stone like in a perfectly molded concert hall, making it hard to tell where it was coming from.

Bryce shined his light around the edge of the space, stopping directly across the cavern. A thin stream of water fell down the rock along the wall, almost translucent in the faint beam from his flashlight. It wasn't a pounding force like the waterfall outside, but a delicate shower, like water flowing over the edge of an expensive infinity pool. He strained his eyes and thought he could see a space behind the film of water, as if the passage he'd traveled might continue. The echoes made it hard to tell, but Bryce thought the humming sound was coming from that side of the cave. It might be from the passage, if it continued past the pool.

He eyed the sides of the cave, hoping to find a foothold or a thin ledge along the rim. He took a careful step, but the rock was slick, and he almost tumbled in. One of his dad's favorite sayings was that the shortest distance between two points was a straight line, and it appeared the only way to the other side of the pool was to wade in.

Bryce stripped off his clothes, except for the bandage around his calf. He stuffed them into his pack. They'd partially dried from the river, and he didn't want them soaked again. Without sunlight, there was no telling how long it would take for his clothes to dry in this cave. He felt foolish skinny-dipping, but there was no reason for modesty. As during most of his time within *Kingdom*, he was completely alone. After a few steps, the bottom dropped away, and Bryce kicked off from the edge while paddling with one arm, working to keep his pack above his head with the other.

The water here was cooler than the river on the surface, but it wasn't freezing. A current flowed around him like a mild jet in a whirlpool tub. His eyes adjusted further to the darkness now that he no longer had his flashlight. He noticed a scattered glow, like fireflies on a warm summer evening at dusk, coming from inside the water. As he reached the center of the pool, the number of glowing lights multiplied. Suddenly there were hundreds of them, thousands maybe, lighting up the water like twinkling Christmas lights. The glow from the water illuminated all the way to the domed ceiling.

Bryce had a mounting sense that something was not right. He kicked harder as the white glow changed to a greenish hue. He felt the colorful organisms moving all around him, leaving behind a slight sting when they brushed his skin, a little like a jellyfish in the ocean. It was almost like a mild pinch of electricity ran through him every time he was hit, but it also seemed to grow stronger. Bryce slid the pack over his shoulders, not caring if it got wet now, and paddled with both arms.

He was nearly to the waterfall, but his progress had slowed. The current was swirling around him like a whirlpool, gaining speed and trying to suck him down. He glanced back at where he'd entered the pool. He saw a large ripple in the water. A fin was cutting through the green glow, moving in a pattern toward the center of the pool.

Bryce fought the urge to freeze up. He struggled to swim harder. He kicked hard, even with his injured leg, stretching his arms out with every stroke to reach the shore. The jolts of energy were constant now, like piranhas were nipping at his skin, drawing at his strength and energy to keep him from reaching the other side.

He didn't dare look back. He wasn't sure what he'd seen behind him, but he had to keep swimming. The shore was only ten feet away now. He could almost touch the rocky edge. As he reached out his arm, something rough and scaly brushed against his right leg. At the touch, his entire body convulsed, his kicking stopped, and for a moment, his head dropped below the surface. It was impossible to tell if something had shocked him or if it had just touched his wound.

Bryce opened his eyes. A long, horrible creature, shaped like an eel but large as a shark, rushed past his face. It circled him then stopped and stared at him with deep, mesmerizing green eyes. Then its mouth cracked open, revealing rows of razor-sharp teeth gleaming through the light-filled water.

Bryce broke from his spell. He swung his pack, striking the creature enough to create a momentary opening. He pulled at the water and, with one last surge, kicked up to the surface, grasping the rocky edge with his fingers. He pulled himself up, his leg burning as it scraped along the rock. The creature leapt up, clamping its mighty jaws onto the open air just as Bryce's foot reached the safety of the ledge.

Bryce collapsed on the rock, gasping for breath. The gentle water cascaded over him like he was under a showerhead. He watched the creature cut in tight circles through the pool, angrily plotting out its next move to get the dinner that had narrowly escaped.

CHAPTER EIGHT

B ryce threw his pack through the open space on the other side of the small waterfall. The humming sound was close now, and was definitely coming from the passage beyond the falls. He stepped through the water and shined his flashlight up a short tunnel, but there was already a light up ahead and around the corner. Was it the surface? That seemed impossible since he'd been descending for a long time. He pulled his clothes from his pack, wrung the water from them the best he could, and got dressed. He trained his flashlight further up the passage and slowly crept toward the light source.

He realized now that the light and the humming were connected. Both grew stronger as he reached the end of the tunnel and came to a very modern-looking glass door. It seemed completely out of place, deep within the ground, and reminded him of the door outside one of the computer labs at Q2, or when he'd visited the computer science department in Lightcap Hall at Tech. But this one also looked like it had been abandoned for decades, its glass cloudy and covered with smudges from dirt and cobwebs. What was it doing here?

When Bryce stepped up to the door, it suddenly slid open. He jumped back at the movement, but then he realized it was just an automatic door, like at the supermarket. He leaned through the doorway and gasped. Even through the dim light, he recognized the space. The room behind the door was the main programming lab back at Q2, or at least it looked just like it. But that was impossible. Was it real, or something else, like a mirage in the desert?

He stepped in and gazed across the space. The dimensions were identical, from the railed platform where he stood, to the rows of computing stations scattered across the wide room, to the glass windows up near the ceiling where Yao had watched and waited. It seemed like a mirror of the real lab back on the mountain. The only noticeable difference was that the place at the front of the room where the giant Eden machine had stood was now empty.

The electronic buzzing was loud now, seeming to come from the rows of dim lights along the ceiling. Bryce walked to where the switches for the lights had been located in the lab back at Q2. He inched the levels higher and the room instantly brightened, significantly reducing the humming sound.

A hint of movement caught his eye near the mainframe. What was that? Bryce crouched and silently peered around the metal railing. He'd been so used to being alone that it

45

hadn't occurred to him that someone else might be in the lab. He waited and then saw it again. It was far away, and while the room was brighter than it had been, the light was still spotty. A figure was at one of the computer stations beside the mainframe. But who?

Bryce took a long breath. He couldn't just hide, especially not after turning the lights on. He gripped the flashlight tightly, ready to use it as a weapon if needed—although it would be of little use if it was a Ranger or something worse. He tiptoed down the metal stairs, his eyes trained on the front of the room. But his foot caught on the bottom step and, for an instant, he lost his balance. He reached out to grab the railing, but his flashlight banged against the metal bar. A clang rang out, and Bryce froze on the last step. He waited for the person to respond, to turn, but nothing happened. Whoever it was didn't move at all.

Bryce loosened his death grip on the railing and walked up the aisle. Each of the workstations looked exactly like the ones in the compound—notebooks, pens, and other office materials were scattered around the desks—but the monitors were dark. A thick film of dust covered everything, like there'd been a sudden evacuation or everyone had just disintegrated.

He remembered the last time he'd walked down this aisle—when he, Charlie, and Rachel had entered the lab that night to use the Eden machine. It was the last he'd seen of the real world, before Heather had gunned Charlie down, and when he and Rachel were flung across dimensions and into this place. The image of Rachel crept back into his mind, but he tried to focus on what was in front of him.

He stopped at the edge of the mainframe, suddenly recognizing the figure. It was Fitz. But at the same time, it wasn't. He was toiling away at his computer, every detail the same, right down to the creaking of his chair under his enormous weight and the assortment of trash and leftover food containers littered about.

Bryce was close enough to be seen, even by someone deep in concentration. But the giant man didn't look up from his workstation. He wasn't real. It had to be some form of hologram. Bryce sank to the floor, suddenly feeling dizzy. His brain was spinning with too many questions. Why would Q2 hide a copy of the programming lab deep underground? Why could he see the hologram of Fitz?

He walked up to the hologram and peered at the screen over Fitz's shoulder. What was he working on so diligently? Bryce watched as the fat man banged away at the keyboard, quickly recognizing the patterns on the screen. He was programming, entering new code sequences very similar to the ones Bryce and his team had done for Heather and Q2. Fitz was building something, or at least altering some existing code structure.

Bryce turned back to the workstations around the room. Fitz's station was the only computer monitor illuminated, but did that mean it was the only one that worked? He walked to one of the other workstations and discovered it was an actual machine, not a hologram. He sat and pressed the computer's power button. For a second nothing happened, but then a blurry, green glow came from the monitor. Bryce wiped away the dust with his sleeve as the monitor slowly came to life.

He stared in disbelief. It was a direct access port into the Q2 mainframe, similar to the one in the communications device he'd accessed on the Central Plateau to message Zach. If he logged in, would it signal his presence to Q2? Could he communicate again with Zach, or reach out to Hendrickson and Tyler? There were so many unknowns.

Bryce glanced at Fitz's hologram, remembering the repulsive man's maniacal eyes when he'd activated the Eden machine. They were madmen—Fitz, Yao, and the whole lot of them. Bryce felt an anger rising up inside. He had to take action, go on the offensive, and bring them all down.

He was tired of running and waiting for others to rescue him. He'd tried sitting still, and Rachel had died. He'd tried warning Zach, but that nearly got his brother killed. Hiding would only bring more of the same—days, months, years even, stuck in this strange, terrible place.

He wanted no more of a life like that. He had to force a way back home, and if that was impossible, at least bring an end to all of Yao's horrible plans and prevent him from hurting the people and the world he loved.

Bryce logged into the mainframe with a renewed energy. He knew he had to work quickly. At first he glanced at Fitz's hologram every couple minutes, but he soon became absorbed in his work. His fingers moved over the keyboard, falling back into that familiar routine of programming lines of code that would carry out the ideas in his head.

A sharp shock jabbed at his fingers, and Bryce jerked his hands back from the keys. A panic shot through him. They'd discovered him. He glanced back at Fitz, but he hadn't changed. The shock had been similar to when he'd been working at the Q2 compound and Tyler had messaged him, somehow cutting through the interface. Could Tyler be monitoring the system and reaching out again with a message?

As he considered the possibilities, an alert appeared in the screen's bottom right corner. His heart skipped a beat. Was it a trap?

Bryce clicked on the blinking alert. He had to chance it. A message box appeared. It was empty at first, but then words slowly formed. "Look up."

He raised his glance from the screen, spinning around in his chair. What did that mean? Fitz was still working at the mainframe, but then to Bryce's right, a flicker appeared at a neighboring workstation. An image slowly came into focus. It was another hologram.

Bryce stared at the face of the person now visible beside him. "Oh my god," he muttered in disbelief. "Is it really you?"

CHAPTER NINE_

M aggie followed Tyler's car to a small parking lot behind Lightcap Hall. Beside them, a wide field of carefully trimmed grass had a painted white circle with a giant letter "H" in the center.

"What are we doing here?" said Zach.

Tyler waved them over to the edge of the grass just as a large, dark green military helicopter roared overhead. They stood and watched as the chopper descended onto the circled "H." The force of the breeze flattened the blades of grass and blew everyone's hair in wild directions.

Andrew turned to Tyler. "You're not serious!" he shouted, as a soldier in fatigues jumped from the helicopter and ran over to them.

"Are you sure about this?" Jess asked her brother.

Tyler nodded confidently and waved them all forward. They jogged toward the soldier and the helicopter, instinc-

50

tively crouching down like in the movies even though the rotors seemed to be far above them.

A pilot with a military-style helmet and headset sat in the cockpit as the other soldier helped the group into the side door, fastened them into seats, and placed headsets over their ears. Zach felt like they were heading off to war, and maybe they were. Maggie sat next to him and reached over and gripped Zach's left hand. With his right, Zach clutched at the edge of the seat as the helicopter lifted off the ground unevenly. But it quickly leveled and climbed higher.

Maggie's grip on Zach's hand was like a vice as they rose into the sky. He realized that he was holding his breath, and he forced himself to exhale. Zach looked out the window and saw Tech's campus rush away beneath them, but then nothing but trees, scattered across the mountain like tiny green sticks, were visible.

"Everybody all right back there?" a voice called through the headset. Zach suddenly realized they could communicate. Everyone had been so tense leaving the ground, they hadn't uttered a word.

Zach nodded, but his throat was dry and he couldn't speak.

"Yeah," Tyler replied, looking to each member of the group for confirmation.

"This is crazy!" Andrew shouted.

Jess nudged him. "You don't have to scream. We can all hear you loud and clear."

Andrew frowned. "Sorry."

"Where are we going?" Zach finally asked.

"Arrival in Quantico at fifteen hundred hours," said the pilot. "About ninety minutes."

Maggie gradually loosened her grip. She let out a short laugh and glanced over at Zach. "I've never been in a helicopter, have you?"

He shook his head. "No. And this wasn't how I pictured my first time."

"It takes a little getting used to," came Tyler's voice. "Sit back and relax, we'll be there before you know it."

Zach watched the scenery fly by below him for a few minutes, but then he felt queasy in his stomach, like when he used to read on family car trips. He rested his head back against the seat, closed his eyes, and took deep breaths. Crazy or not, there was nothing he could do about it now.

An hour and a half later, the helicopter touched down in a marked corner of a parking lot at a large office building complex. The pilot killed the engine, and the soldier came around to open the side doors and help them to the ground. Zach's legs felt wobbly as they hit the pavement, but he followed the others in a line behind the soldier across the parking lot. They entered one of several identical-looking buildings, all with exteriors of light gray-colored cement and row after row of square, recessed windows.

At the security station inside the lobby, they moved one by one through a series of scanning machines like the metal detectors at the airport. Andrew had to go through twice because he hadn't fully emptied his pockets. On the other side, the group was handed ID badges that clipped to their shirts and directed to a small waiting room with chairs.

The soldier asked Tyler to follow him. "I'll be right back," said Tyler. "I promise."

Andrew leaned in close. "This is nuts. Do you think we're under arrest? Were any of you read your rights? They have to do that, don't they? I was just kidding about the nukes, you know. But I'll bet—"

Jess slugged him in the shoulder. "Shut *up*, will you!" She shook her head. "God, it's like you don't have an off switch."

Andrew was about to offer a defense, but Zach gave him a warning look and he finally seemed to get it and closed his mouth.

After a few minutes, Tyler appeared in the doorway and waved them into the hall. They quickly stood and joined him.

"What's going on?" asked Zach.

"Like I said," answered Tyler. "Someone's been captured."

"Who?" asked Andrew. "Besides us?"

"Professor Hendrickson said he'll explain it to us in a minute," replied Tyler. He walked them to the elevator bank, where they crowded into an elevator and dropped three levels underground before the doors opened. Another uniformed guard stood outside a door just up the hallway. Tyler showed his ID, and the man opened the door and waved them through to a conference room with a large mirror covering most of the far wall.

The door soon opened and Hendrickson walked in. "I'm glad you made it."

"We didn't really have a choice," answered Zach.

"Sorry about that. Things are moving quickly, there have been a lot of developments even since we saw each other this morning."

"Are we in trouble?" asked Jess.

The professor shook his head. "No, but the general wants to speak with you."

Andrew caught his breath. "General Weber?" he asked nervously.

"No, General George Washington," said Jess, rolling her eyes. "He's come back from the dead to tell you you're stupid."

Andrew's mouth dropped open. "Hey, I don't know what your problem is…"

Tyler shot his sister a look, and she sighed and backed off.

Hendrickson nodded at Andrew. "Yes, General Weber."

"Tyler said you captured someone," Maggie said. "Who is it?"

The professor stood and walked to the mirror on the wall. He pressed a button and the glass instantly turned clear, revealing a window into another room. It was smaller than the one they sat in, with just a couple chairs and a metal table. Zach recognized the setup from TV—it was an interrogation room.

"Whoa," muttered Andrew.

"It's a one-way mirror," explained Hendrickson. "We can see them, but they can't see us."

Everyone stood and walked closer to the glass as a door opened in the other room. Two soldiers entered with a woman in handcuffs. She was an adult, but much younger than Zach's mom. Her blonde hair was uncombed, and she seemed disheveled. But it was easy to see that she was really pretty, for a grown-up, at least. The woman sat in a chair on one side of the table while the two soldiers remained standing near the door.

Andrew glanced at Zach, a slight grin on his face, but Zach shook his head.

"Give it a break, you two," groaned Jess.

"Who is that?" asked Maggie.

Hendrickson turned and looked at them. "The name on her identification says Jocelyn Rogers; however, that's likely an alias. The FBI believes her true identity is Heather Avanair, a scientist and programmer for Q2. She's been on the run ever since we raided their mountain compound. As I think you've heard, the rest of Q2's senior operatives have disappeared, likely already out of the country. But Ms. Avanair here seems to have missed her departure connection."

"Where was she?" asked Tyler.

"They pulled her over coming out of the Chesapeake Bay Bridge-Tunnel heading toward Norfolk. She likely had a vessel waiting for her in the port. We're fortunate that state police scanned the license plate. Her vehicle reported as stolen three days ago in Durham."

"What are you going to do to her?" Zach asked.

"The FBI and several military contacts on General

Weber's team have been questioning her," said the professor, "but I'm told, so far, she's not talking."

Zach tried to follow what Hendrickson was saying. "So if they're interrogating her, what do you need us here for? We don't know anything about her."

"The general would like to speak with you," said Hendrickson.

"Me?" said Zach.

"All of you. They're trying to tie together loose ends."

Maggie stepped closer to the glass. "There's something familiar about that woman. I feel like I've seen her somewhere before."

"That's unlikely," said Hendrickson. "We're pretty sure she was operating at the Q2 compound, perhaps organizing some of their programming databases. Though it's possible she may have worked with recruits like Bryce."

Their conference room door swung open suddenly, and three men in military uniforms stepped into the room. In the middle was General Weber. His short haircut, stocky build, and chiseled jaw made him look like he'd been cast for the role of 'military general' by a Hollywood producer.

"Have a seat, everyone."

They snapped out of their surprise and quickly scrambled to the nearest open chairs. The two other soldiers remained against the wall at near-attention, ready to spring into action if the general snapped his fingers. One of them pressed a switch in the wall and the window to the interrogation room returned to its mirrored state.

General Weber glanced at Hendrickson. "This is everyone?"

The professor nodded. "Yes, sir."

"Very well. Let's get started then." He sat in the head chair, placed his hands flat on the table, and stared at them solemnly like he was about to provide the location of secret German bunkers before a World War II bombing raid.

"Kids, I called you here because we have a serious situation. Professor Hendrickson has briefed me on your involvement in the JOSHUA project, and while this is extremely unusual, these are unusual times. The security of your nation, and quite possibly the world as we know it, may rest on how we move forward. It is your responsibility —it is your duty as Americans, to take this seriously. We don't know how much has already compromised our ability to control the outcomes, but the more we do know, the greater chance we have of minimizing the damage."

Zach knew he should sit quietly, but he couldn't help it. He slipped his hand into the air. Hendrickson discreetly shook his head, but the general had already seen the hand. He raised his eyebrows at Zach as though he was a man not used to being interrupted.

"Yes?"

Zach swallowed hard. "I'm sorry, sir. I don't mean to be disrespectful. But what about my brother? Bryce is still on the other side of the digital bridge. What are you doing to bring him home?"

General Weber's face took on a practiced expression that said he was carefully considering the question. He folded his hands in front of him. "You can trust me when I tell you, son, that we are taking the matter of your brother's disappearance very seriously."

"He didn't disappear," said Maggie quickly. "He's inside *Kingdom*."

The general glanced at Hendrickson and then around the table. "I understand this is particularly hard for all of you as family and friends. We are committed to bringing home every American. But this has turned into a situation that is much greater than…" He looked back at Hendrickson for help.

"Bryce Pearson, sir."

"Yes, of course. It's much greater than Bryce. We believe that when the bridge was activated, it may have interrupted the normal cosmic rhythms, creating an atmospheric regression that could produce dramatic changes to our environment and every living person. Until we better understand the effects of these abnormalities, we have no choice but to postpone any rescue operations."

Zach tried to process what he was hearing. "What do you mean *postpone*?"

"You want to leave him?" said Maggie, her voice straining.

The general held up his hand. "No one said anything about abandoning him. But we need to methodically research the data we've been collecting to ensure that reopening the bridge will not create additional damage. It's for the good of the nation."

Zach dropped his head. They were going to leave Bryce over there. This couldn't be happening.

The general rose from his seat and glanced at the other two soldiers. "These gentlemen are part of our behavioral science team. They'll interview each of you to ensure we have every possible detail for our analysis." He looked over at Zach and tried a weak smile. "The more we understand these phenomena, the better chance we have of ensuring your brother's safe return."

The general nodded for Professor Hendrickson to follow him into the hallway as the other two soldiers stepped forward to the table.

"If you could all follow us," said one of the men, "we'll be interviewing each of you individually. The others can wait more comfortably in the room next to security."

Zach tried to stand, but his legs felt stuck. His entire body was numb. Jess reached over and gently tugged on his arm. "Come on, Zach, we'll figure this out."

He reluctantly stood and walked to the doorway. As they filed into the hall, the door to the neighboring interrogation room opened. Two guards escorted the woman, Heather Avanair, into the hallway. Zach and the others stopped and stared, intrigued by the woman as though she were a new animal species at the zoo. What did she know? What were they going to do with her?

"Move to the side, please," said one of the soldiers as the group approached.

The woman stared right at Zach and Maggie, standing together on the right side of the hallway. She dragged her feet, slowing to a stop right in front of them. A knowing grin filled her face.

"A pity about Bryce. He was really such a… catch." Her voice had an accent, Australian maybe.

Zach's mouth dropped open in surprise, but Maggie didn't flinch. "What did you say?" she snapped back.

Heather leaned closer to Maggie. "He was such a bright young mind. It's such a shame to see him lost so young. There was such potential ahead of him. So many… opportunities."

All at once it seemed like something exploded within Maggie. She lunged at the woman with a flurry of fists and screams. "Don't you talk about him, you hear me? What did you do to him? I'll kill you, do you understand?"

The soldiers sprang into action, two grabbing Maggie in a shoulder lock to restrain her, while the others pulled Heather Avanair away from the attack.

"Maggie!" the professor shouted. "Stop!"

It was all Zach could do to not just stand and gape at what had just happened, but he turned and tried to calm Maggie down. He'd never seen her so upset. It was like all the months of anguish from Bryce's disappearance had erupted in fury at the woman.

"Get her out of here!" shouted the general, motioning for the soldiers to take Heather Avanair away. He turned to Maggie. "I don't know where you think you are, but another outburst like that and I'll lock you up as well. Understood, young lady?"

Maggie didn't answer right away, but she stopped flailing. "Okay," she said finally, shaking off the soldiers' grip.

Zach, Maggie, and Andrew were led to the waiting room to calm down while Tyler and then Jess were sent in for the first interviews. When the trio reached the waiting room chairs, Maggie burst into tears, burying her head in Zach's shoulder and throwing her arms around him. "Why is all this happening?" she sobbed.

Zach had felt most of the same emotions that Maggie showed in the hallway. But instead of letting them out, he felt them burrowing deep within him like a cancer, eating at his core bit by bit. He wanted to say it was going to be okay, that they would find Bryce and bring him home. But he wasn't so sure anymore. He wasn't sure about anything.

He squeezed Maggie tighter, shook his head, and whispered the only words that didn't seem like a lie. "I don't know. I just don't know."

CHAPTER TEN_

I t was a quiet ride back home, even in the helicopter.
After several hours of interviews, no one seemed to feel
much like talking. Since it was late, instead of flying back to
Tech, General Weber had them transported straight to
Milton. They landed on a small helipad behind the new
hospital. A dark, hulking Suburban delivered them one by
one to their houses. Tyler was returning separately with the
professor, and he agreed to drive Maggie's Explorer back to
her house the next day.

They'd phoned home from the waiting room and
explained to their parents that they'd been tied up even
longer than planned at Tech with Jess's brother. It was kind
of in the same zip code as the truth, but not really. Zach
had been holding his parents at arm's length for a long time.
He knew things had to change. Maybe this was going to be
what pushed it over the edge.

His mom had been close to tears on the phone, and

while Zach assured her he was safe, he didn't know what else to say. Even if he could explain that a military general needed to chat with him at Quantico, that wouldn't cut it. After everything that had happened with Bryce, he didn't blame his parents for being worried, or even suspecting that their other son might not come home at all. You look at the world differently when you've been through what they had.

Even though it wasn't a long ride, Andrew and Jess both fell asleep in the far back seat of the Suburban as it navigated through Milton's quiet streets. Zach was content to rest as well, but Maggie seemed to want to chat. "I'm sorry I lost it back there," she whispered.

"You don't have to apologize," Zach answered. "Anyone would have acted the same way."

"I know getting mad won't help anything."

"Maybe it will."

She glanced at him, her face reflecting the glow of streetlights as they passed the high school. "What do you mean?"

"So they don't forget about him," said Zach. "I doubt Bryce is their biggest concern. You heard Weber. He couldn't even remember Bryce's name. If we stop pushing, they might leave him over there forever."

Maggie let out a long breath. "You know they still might, even if we push."

"Yeah." Zach liked that he and Maggie had always said it like it was. As much as he didn't want to face that truth, he knew she was right.

Maggie stared out the window. "Every time I think

about that woman in the hallway, my skin crawls. I've never wanted to strangle someone so much in my life. There was something about the way she looked at us. The tone in her voice."

Zach nodded. "She had an evil confidence."

"Exactly."

"Did you really recognize her?"

"She looked very familiar," Maggie said. "I just can't place her."

"She seemed to know about Bryce. Maybe they'll cut her a deal to get her talking. She might tell the government something useful that will bring Bryce back."

"Maybe." Maggie glanced at the backseat and chuckled. Jess's head was resting peacefully on Andrew's shoulder. "I should take a picture."

"She'd kill you," said Zach, laughing.

Maggie reached over and squeezed his hand. "Thanks for staying awake with me."

Zach smiled. "No problem."

Before Zach reached the porch, his mom was opening the front door. She hugged him tightly and walked him into the living room where his dad was sitting on the couch. His dad glanced up at the clock on the mantle above the fireplace. He turned back at Zach like he was about to scold him, but he just stood and wrapped him in a long hug.

"I'm sorry it's so late," said Zach. "I didn't mean to worry you."

His mom shook her head and put her index finger to

his lips. "Not tonight. I'm just glad you're safe." She nodded to the couch and had Zach sit between the two of them.

The TV was paused, like they'd been watching it together while they were waiting for him to come home. It was unusual these days to see them spending time together, but Zach recognized the video. They were watching one of Bryce's track meets from his sophomore year. Zach didn't know if it was a positive step that they'd broken out the old videos, or if it just made the hurt worse for them to see Bryce's face on the screen. He seemed so close, so real... so not stuck in a faraway land.

Zach often wondered if his knowing the truth made it easier or harder than his parents' not knowing at all. He'd decided that both had their drawbacks and that the better choice was having Bryce sitting there on the couch. Everything like it used to be. The four of them a family again.

Zach glanced at the screen. "I think that's the race where Bart Schofield dropped the baton in the anchor leg, isn't it? The one against East Mason."

His dad nodded. "I think you're right. Nearly created a five-lane pileup on the track."

"I can't remember, did Bryce get stuck in that?" asked his mom.

"No, he was running second that year," Zach answered. "Coach Simmons had been out for a month after his gallbladder surgery, and Mr. Rodriguez didn't think Bryce was ready to run anchor."

His mom groaned. "Oh, Mr. Rodriguez. I nearly forgot about him. I never liked that man much."

Zach chuckled. "I think he was the only person in Milton who didn't think Bryce walked on water."

She slapped Zach's knee playfully. "That's not true. Your brother was good at a lot of things, but Lord knows he wasn't perfect."

"You can say that again," said Zach.

"He was always running late for things," said his mom. "He chewed with his mouth open. And do you remember how bad his socks smelled? I don't know where he got such stinky feet, but it wasn't from my side of the family."

His dad frowned. "You're saying my family smells?"

His mom grinned. "Not in so many words."

"He ran over the apricot tree I planted in the backyard with the riding mower, do you remember that?" said his dad. "Seared it clean off. Broke the drive belt, dented the blades. Mower never did work properly after that."

Zach looked over at him. "Is that why you got rid of it?"

His mom shook her head. "That's the excuse he used to get rid of it. The reality is he'd been eying Jack Harper's John Deere across the street for years."

Zach raised his eyebrows. "Is that true, Dad?"

"I'm sticking with my story," he muttered, then stared back at Bryce's smiling face plastered across the screen.

"I miss him," whispered Zach. "It's just not the same without him here." His dad stretched his arm around his shoulders and gave a quick glance across the couch to his mom.

Zach sensed a tension hanging in the air, like something

needed to be said. "What is it?" he asked nervously, when no one spoke.

"Zach," said his mom, "we need to talk about some things."

That queasy feeling that he now knew too well returned to his stomach. It had been such a long day. He didn't know if he could handle anything else.

"Son, you know that things have been difficult at work," said his dad.

Zach nodded. "Yeah, I know." His dad had taken a new job shortly before Bryce's disappearance, but his bosses hadn't seemed to appreciate him as much as the bosses at his old job. His new manager, Frank, had given him a tough time about nearly everything, and despite some new sales prospects with a client in Omaha, things had recently taken a downturn. Zach didn't know the details, but more than once he'd overheard his dad talking to Frank on the phone in his office about dealing with the client's complaints.

"Despite doing everything I could to make my client out in Omaha happy," said his dad, "they announced this morning that they're pulling all their business."

Zach closed his eyes.

"That was your dad's biggest account," his mom added.

"I know, Mom." Zach saw that his dad was trying to keep a positive expression, but he wasn't succeeding. It looked like he'd aged twenty years since everything with his job and Bryce had started. "Why would they do that, Dad? You've been working so hard." Despite everything, his dad had still been flying back and forth to Omaha every week to meet with the client and answer their questions.

His dad nodded. "I have, you're right. But somehow they've gotten stuck on some misinformation… they're claiming that I didn't deliver on my promises. They have these contracts, that I never prepared, that show we didn't meet deadlines… it's hard to understand."

"Someone's spreading lies," said his mom, reaching across Zach to put her hand on Dad's leg. "We know you did nothing wrong."

Zach looked back at his dad. "But you'll get another account, right?"

His dad bit his lip. "It's not going to work out this time. Frank's agreed to give me thirty days to close out my accounts and look for something else."

"Another new job?" Zach's voice was rising. "But you just did that!"

"I know, Zach, and I don't want you to worry about it. I'll take care of it, but we thought you should know…" His voice trailed off, but Zach could tell there was something else.

"What?" Zach asked. His dad was a proud man, and he knew it wasn't easy for him to admit failure. His own parents, Grandma and Grandpa Pearson, were blue-collar folks who'd taught him the value of hard work. Providing for one's family was important. A man wasn't supposed to lose his job. Or his son.

Zach felt his phone buzz with a text, but he ignored it and kept his eyes trained on his dad.

"You know that times were already tight financially. I've gone over the numbers a hundred times, and well… it's just not adding up. We'll have to put the house on the market."

Zach felt the numbness seep back into his brain. Why was this happening to them? This was the only house he'd ever lived in. It was where Bryce had lived. He couldn't imagine anywhere else.

His mom forced a smile. "You know, with just three of us, we don't really need all this space. There are some very nice condos over on the west side of town. Lisa at work told me her sister has a beautiful three-story townhome with a garage."

And that was when Zach lost it. The floodgates opened up. He couldn't hold it in any longer. He buried his head in his mom's arms and wept, realizing that this might be how their family was from now on.

"We're still here for you, Zach," whispered his dad. "No matter what happens, that'll never change."

Zach nodded and gradually pulled back. He saw that his mom was staring at his head. "Honey…" she started. "What's going on with your hair? I thought that white spot had grown out, but I see some white down here in the roots… are you dying it?"

And right then, Zach knew he had to tell them.

There was no point in holding it back any longer. All his defenses were down, and he couldn't keep it to himself, despite what Hendrickson, Tyler, or even General Weber had said. They needed to know the truth. They deserved to know the truth, about Bryce, about everything Zach had been doing lately, about the whole messy business.

He took a long breath, then slid onto the floor so he could turn and see them both at once. "I need to tell you guys some things, too."

They both stared at him intently, as if they thought they'd missed some key detail with Bryce and were determined not to do it again. His mom gripped the throw pillow on her lap so tightly her knuckles turned white.

"Remember the day that Bryce went missing?"

His dad cocked his head. "Zach, of course."

"What about it, honey?" asked his mom.

Zach swallowed hard. He'd rehearsed it in his mind so many times, but now that he was sitting with them, his mind was almost blank. He didn't know where to begin. "I saw him."

"Saw who?" asked his mom. "Bryce?"

"Zach, what are you talking about?" His dad leaned forward over the edge of the couch as if he hadn't heard right.

But then headlights flashed through the front window. A vehicle pulled into the driveway. Another stopped along the road in front of the house. Zach's parents still stared at him like they were oblivious to the lights.

"Son, what were you saying about Bryce?" said his dad. "When did you see him?"

Zach turned and saw shadows on the grass. Men were coming up the walk toward the house. They were almost to the porch. Zach didn't have to think about it. He immediately knew what was happening. They were coming for him. When he stood and turned to the door, it finally seemed to break his parents' trance.

"Zach, who's out there?" his mom called.

He just looked back at them and tried to hold in the tears. "I'm sorry, guys," he cried. "I don't know what to do."

His dad rose from the couch and walked to the door as Zach's cell phone rang. Maggie was calling. He also saw three missed texts from Jess.

They're coming for you, Zach. Tyler says Gen Weber is pulling you in.

Then the doorbell rang and everything was a blur.

Several men in suits flashed their identification badges and strode right past his dad into the foyer. His mom gripped Zach's arm, tears streaming down her cheeks. They both demanded answers, even as the men led Zach out the front door and onto the porch. His dad struggled to get past the men, to grab Zach's hand, but two other men appeared and blocked his path. His dad slipped on the grass and tumbled down.

As they led Zach to the street, he watched his father, as if in slow motion, rolling twice down the slope next to the porch. His mom was screaming and trying to help him up. One of the men beside Zach opened a car door and pushed Zach's head down, maneuvering him into the back seat. The final image in his mind was that of his parents huddled together on the grass, staring at the nameless men taking away their last remaining son.

CHAPTER ELEVEN

"Hang on a sec, what do you mean they took him?" Andrew stared into the trees, as if squadrons of soldiers were about to storm the field.

"I mean they took him," said Jess, leaning against the boulder.

"Like under arrest?"

"I don't think so." She stared out at the withered grass being blown around the barren field by a cold breeze. "My brother sent me a text last night that said I had to warn Zach that officers from General Weber's group were coming to take him back to Quantico."

Andrew threw a stick over the boulder. "But we were all just there yesterday. Why would they let us go home, only to turn around and decide to take him back? That doesn't make any sense."

"Ty said they found the security tapes that showed Zach

coming back across the bridge. I think he's in some kind of quarantine."

"Quarantine?"

"Yeah, you know, locked up in isolation so he can't expose anyone else."

Andrew shook his head. "Expose us to what? He's been with us for months. If he's infected with something, then so are the rest of us, no?"

"If it's contagious."

"There's nothing wrong with him, I mean, apart from that thing with his hair."

Jess nodded. "You and I know that, but I don't think Weber will be quite so trusting. Ty says they're worried about potential side effects from crossing the digital bridge and being in the virtual world."

"Like what, some kind of radiation or something?"

"Maybe."

Andrew stopped and considered this for a moment. "What's the deal with his hair turning white like that, anyway? Do you think it's something bad?"

Jess shook her head. "This whole thing is bad. But his hair? I don't think so."

"Then what is it?"

"Stress, maybe. My dad said anxiety can do weird things to people."

Andrew waved his hand. "What does he know."

"He's a doctor, remember?" said Jess, rolling her eyes.

"Whatever." He looked over his shoulder at the woods

that blocked the view to Zach's neighborhood. "I thought Maggie was coming."

"She must still be with Zach's parents. She said they weren't told very much last night when he was taken away. They've contacted their US senator to try to get to the bottom of things, but who knows what will happen. Maggie said they were a wreck."

"No doubt. My mom would completely freak if that happened to me."

Jess nodded. "Mine too. Can you imagine?" She glanced around the field, the dead stalks of grass folded over and dormant in the cold weather. "So this is where Zach saw the fox and the Ranger the first time, right?"

Andrew nodded. "He said he saw the fox hologram right near this boulder, and then the Sportsman talked to him over there." He pointed to a part of the field closer to the road.

Jess bit her lip. "I feel like we're missing something."

"I don't think there's anything else out here," said Andrew. "This field was just where Bryce placed the fox to get Zach's attention so he'd see the message."

"Message?" asked Jess.

"Yeah, don't you remember? The fox was a sign so that when Zach saw it again inside *Kingdom*, he'd follow it to the cave in the canyon wall. That's where Bryce hid the video with the message." Andrew peered at her suspiciously. "You all right? You know all this. That's how we learned about Hendrickson in the first place."

Jess snapped her head up. "That's it!"

Andrew raised his eyebrows. "It is? You mean Professor Hendrickson?"

"No, a message!"

"Zach already found it in the cave."

Jess started tapping her foot in the dirt excitedly. "No, not that one. You said the fox showed up to lead Zach to a message, right?"

"Yeah…"

"And the other day, when we were playing in *Kingdom*, we saw the same fox again."

"Sure," answered Andrew. "By the river."

Jess's eyes bulged like they were about to pop out of her face. "Oh my gosh, it's so obvious! How did I not think of this before?"

Andrew looked at her with his head crooked. "Um, I don't know…"

Jess opened her mouth wide. "What if he was trying to give us a message?"

"The fox?"

"No! I mean, yes, but Bryce… through the fox. Did we ever look for a message?"

Andrew thought about it for a moment and then shook his head. "No, I think Zach was too excited about seeing the fox and how it meant that Bryce was safe. Then we hid when the Rangers stormed by. But I didn't see a message, just the fox."

Jess was pacing now in front of the boulder. "Was Zach still using the capture card to record all of our game missions?"

"Yeah. I think so," Andrew replied. "He wanted to have a record, just in case. I'm pretty sure he kept saving them even though we never found anything."

"Until this!" Jess tugged on his arm. "Come on, we need to go watch that recording."

"Now?"

She sighed. "Yes, *now*. Where is it?"

Andrew nodded back toward the woods. "It's in Zach's room, but I don't think his parents will want us traipsing through their house the morning after he was taken and all..."

But Jess was already jogging across the field toward the trail to Zach's house. "We have no choice," she called over her shoulder. "We have to see that tape."

Andrew sighed. "Okay... I guess we're going now."

* * *

Jess rang the doorbell as she stood next to Andrew on Zach's front porch, and then again a few seconds later after no one answered. They finally heard voices and footsteps, and then Zach's dad was standing before them, but with a distant stare in his eyes.

"Andrew," he said, before he nodded at Jess.

"Jess," she prompted him. She could see Mrs. Pearson sitting on the couch with Maggie in the living room.

"Hi, Mr. P," said Andrew. "Sorry to bother you."

Zach's dad attempted to brighten his expression. "What? You know you're never a bother, Andrew. Maggie's here too." He moved to the side. "Come in. We were just talking about the boys."

"Thanks," said Jess, as they stepped inside.

"Hi, guys," said Maggie, waving from the couch. "Sorry I didn't make it over. We got busy talking here."

Mrs. Pearson jumped up and gave Andrew a big hug. It was easy to see that she'd been crying.

Jess pulled Maggie aside. "We need to talk to you."

Andrew unfolded himself from Mrs. Pearson's embrace. "Would you mind if we look in Zach's room for a few minutes? I think I left my controller in there, and we need to check something on his computer."

"His computer?" asked Mr. Pearson, like he'd never heard of one. "Of course. Whatever you need, Andrew."

"Thanks, Mr. P." Andrew led the way down the hallway to Zach's bedroom. Jess and Maggie sat on the bed while he picked through some wires and adaptors on Zach's book-shelf and then booted up the computer.

"They're beside themselves," said Maggie, shaking her head. "And I don't know what to tell them…it's just awful."

"I'm sure," said Jess. "I can't imagine how they must feel right now."

Maggie looked at Andrew working at the desk. "What's going on? Did you find something?"

"Not yet," said Jess, "but we have a hunch."

"*She* has a hunch," Andrew called over his shoulder as the wall monitor turned on. Andrew scrolled through the input menus until he pulled up a list of sessions.

"Got it," said Andrew. He clicked on the most recent

date, and a video appeared on the monitor. It showed the beginning of their round that day in *Kingdom*.

"You recorded yourselves playing the game?" asked Maggie, trying to catch up.

"Yeah," said Jess, nodding at the monitor. "Skip to the end, by the river."

"What are we looking for?" Maggie asked.

"She thinks we missed something," said Andrew, as the avatars jumped back and forth in super-speed across the screen.

"A message," explained Jess. "There had to be a reason why the fox showed up by the river."

"You don't think it was Bryce?" said Maggie hesitantly.

Jess shook her head. "I think it was him, or at least he sent it. But there has to be more to why it was there. Something we didn't see the first time. It's the only thing that makes sense." She pointed at the monitor when the surging river appeared. "There, stop it."

Andrew slowed the recording to normal speed. They watched as their game avatars marched through the field and stopped along the riverbank. Maggie let out a squeal when the fox appeared at the top of the frame.

Andrew froze the video. "There he is." The fox was stepping out from behind a group of bushes further up the riverbank. He started the video again, and they watched the fox move toward them but then freeze when a flurry of activity sounded from the field as the Rangers approached.

"Keep watching the fox," said Jess, pointing at the

screen. It ran back toward the bush then turned and stared back at them. "Stop it right there."

Andrew paused the video, leaving the fox's mesmerizing green eyes locked in their direction. "I still don't see anything."

"Where does it go next?" asked Maggie.

Andrew let the video continue, and they watched the fox scramble behind the bushes and out of sight as their group's avatars jumped beneath the overhang of the riverbank to hide from the Rangers. It was impossible to see where the fox had gone.

"I hate to say 'I told you so,'" said Andrew, "but I did."

Jess ignored him and kept staring at the screen. "Fast-forward to after we left the hiding spot," she instructed. The Rangers stormed off and soon their game players were walking up the riverbank to where the fox had been standing.

"Just like before," said Andrew. "The fox ran away when the Rangers came. I don't blame him, either."

"Stop," shouted Maggie. "Go back."

"What?" asked Andrew, pausing and then rewinding the video several frames.

Maggie leaped up from the bed and moved next to the monitor. "Right there. What's that on the sand?"

"You mean the tracks?" asked Andrew. "It's from the fox. Even avatars in *Kingdom* leave them. I don't think it's a big deal—"

No," said Maggie, pointing at the screen. "Behind the tracks. It almost looks like…"

"Writing," said Jess.

Maggie turned to her. "You see it too?"

"Maybe," said Jess, joining Maggie close to the screen. "I can't tell. Andrew, can you pan up in the video?"

He chuckled and shook his head. "Sorry, this isn't like the movies. We can only see what's on the video."

"What about the opposite camera angle view," said Jess. "I know *Kingdom* has that."

Andrew nodded. "Yeah, of course it does. But only when we're playing the game. This is just a recording of what we saw at the time. We didn't use that other angle, so it didn't record."

Jess groaned and fell back to the bed. "You're right. Then we'll never see it."

"Why don't we just go back?" asked Maggie.

"I told you," said Andrew, "we didn't record it. This is all we can see."

Maggie shook her head. "No, I mean right now. Can't we go into the game and go to that same place by the river?"

Andrew sat for a second, trying to think of a reason they couldn't, but then he nodded. "Yeah, I don't see why not. We already accessed that level, so it shouldn't be that hard to pull it back up. But I don't know if anything from that day will still be here."

Jess glared at him. "Just do it, will you?" She turned to Maggie. "That's a great idea."

"Thanks." Maggie grinned. "Bryce always said I would make a great gamer."

Andrew switched the monitor over to the live game

input and booted up a round. He selected the options for the same mission they'd been on before. Soon they'd retraced their steps and their game avatars were walking up the riverbank.

"I think he was right up here," said Jess, moving toward a patch of green bushes.

"Hopefully we don't encounter any Rangers this time," said Andrew.

"Where did you see that writing?" Jess asked.

"Just past those bushes," Maggie answered, moving back next to the screen while the others operated their controllers. "Stop, right there." She put her finger on the screen near some lines in the sandy bank and squinted her eyes. "What is that?"

"It looks like an arrow," said Andrew.

"It's pointing at the side of the riverbank, but all I see is mud," said Jess.

"What if it's pointing over it?" asked Maggie. "Can you jump back up to the field?"

Andrew's avatar jumped up to the wide grassy field on the other side of the riverbank with Jess's close behind. Jess pointed to an object in the middle of the field. "What about that?"

"You mean that rock?" said Andrew.

"Doesn't it look familiar?" asked Jess, her eyes widening.

Andrew ran toward the gray object standing alone in the field. "No way..." he muttered. It looked exactly like the one they'd been leaning against in the real field outside.

"There has to be something there," said Jess. "It's too big of a coincidence."

Maggie nodded. "Can you walk around it?"

Andrew circled to the back of the boulder, moving as close as he could.

"Right there," said Maggie, pointing at the rock. "Those are words. What does it say?"

Andrew squinted toward the screen, then pressed a button on his controller that zoomed in on the rock. Sure enough, someone had scrawled a message across the back of the stone. "Midnight. Sunday. Power," he read.

Jess shook her head. "No, not power. That's a 't,' not a 'p.' It says 'Tower.'"

The three of them stood speechless in Zach's bedroom, staring at the screen.

"Midnight, Sunday?" Andrew said finally. "Like tonight?"

Jess nodded. "I think so. But what tower does it mean?" She looked back at Maggie, who'd slid onto the edge of the bed with a faraway look in her eyes. "Do you know where there's a tower?"

"Yes." Maggie nodded slowly. "I do."

"If my mom checks my room and sees my bed is empty, she's going to call the cops," said Andrew, leaning forward from the back seat. "Plus, it's a school night. Did you know she nearly locked me in my room after Bryce went missing? She practically had a heart attack this afternoon when Mrs. P called and told her Zach had been hauled away."

"Does she normally check your bed at midnight?" asked Jess from the passenger seat.

Andrew thought about it for a moment. "No."

"Then don't worry about it."

Maggie turned her Explorer into an empty parking lot and came to a stop.

"We're going to the VFW Hall?" asked Andrew. "I thought we were looking for a tower."

Maggie glanced back and forth and then reversed and rolled back out onto the street. "No, I must have passed the road." She retraced their path past the fishing pond on the left and then slowed along a section of woods. "There it is."

They turned onto an unmarked dirt trail, the SUV's suspension bouncing over the potholes. "This isn't a road," Andrew muttered, staring out the side windows at the tall shadows of the trees all around them. "Are you sure this is a good idea?"

"Will you shut up?" Jess scolded.

Andrew shook his head. "No, seriously. Think about it. This could all be a trap. It could be, you know, *him*."

"Who?" said Jess.

"The Sportsman. Or another Ranger, or one of the crazies from Q2. We could be driving out here to our deaths."

"If someone wanted to kill us, they'd have done it already," said Jess, matter-of-factly.

Andrew frowned back at her. "That's not very comforting."

"Plus, all the Rangers were pulled back into *Kingdom* when the bridge closed," said Jess.

"We *think* so, but do we *really* know?" asked Andrew.

"We'll just have to take that chance," said Maggie. "We're here." She pointed to a hulking black object hovering near the tops of the barren tree branches. She put the vehicle in park and handed out flashlights.

"Hold on," said Andrew. "Tell me again why you're so sure this is the right place? I thought we agreed Bryce is still stuck inside *Kingdom*? Why would he have us come all the way out here?"

"I just know," replied Maggie. "I can't explain how. Like I said, this is where he brought me the night before he disappeared."

Andrew raised his eyebrows as he tested his flashlight, training the beam on the creepy trees on the other side of the car's window glass. "He brought you *here*?"

Maggie sighed. "Get your mind out of the gutter. This is when he gave me the necklace for our anniversary. We climbed up the water tower and watched the sunset."

"That's sounds romantic," said Jess.

"It was."

Andrew nudged Jess's shoulder. "You know, since we're already out here…"

Jess made a face like she'd just bitten into a lemon. "Ew, gross. Keep dreaming."

"Keep your voices down." Maggie opened her door and stepped out to the path, her feet crunching in fallen leaves that were scattered across the dirt. She kept her flashlight beam low and walked toward the water tower.

"Where are we going?" whispered Andrew, his breath forming a cloud of fog in the cold air in front of him. "Not up there, I hope."

"Shh!" Jess hissed.

When Andrew stepped on a branch a few yards from the Explorer, the crunching wood sounded like an air horn in the stillness of the night. Jess just turned and glared at him. Maggie raised a finger to her lips as they stood and gazed at the tall tower above them.

As they were staring up at the tower, another branch

snapped. Jess glanced back at Andrew, but he held his hands up. "That was not me. I swear."

They peered into the darkness of the forest, the tall tree trunks looming like hundreds of ghostly soldiers standing guard around the tower. Footsteps crunched in the leaves. Someone was coming toward them.

No one moved a muscle as the shadow of a figure appeared between two trees. "Hello?" Jess finally called.

Maggie stepped closer, raising her light. "Bryce? Is that you?"

The figure moved into the edge of the flashlight beam. Maggie's heart sank. It wasn't Bryce. A boy with shaggy red hair who was about Bryce's age stepped toward them. He looked disheveled, as though he hadn't changed clothes in a while, like he might be homeless and living in the woods underneath the water tower.

"Who the hell are you?" called Andrew, shining his light in the guy's face.

"What do you want?" asked Maggie.

The boy raised his arm to cover his eyes. "Dude, mind the beam! Geez."

Andrew hesitated but lowered his flashlight. "What are you doing out here? Did you set us up?"

The boy shook his head. "My name is Charlie. I'm a friend of Bryce's."

Maggie lowered her eyebrows. "How do you know Bryce? Why did you call us out here in the middle of the night?"

Charlie held up his hands in a nonthreatening way. "I'm

not here to hurt you. I'm actually on your side. Let me guess. You're Maggie?"

She tilted her head suspiciously. "That's right."

He looked at Andrew. "But you're not Zach."

"Boy, you're a real genius," jeered Andrew, framing his dark-skinned face with his hands. "Don't you see the family resemblance?"

"We're Zach's friends. This is Andrew, and I'm Jess. But you still haven't told us what you're doing out here or how you know Bryce."

Charlie motioned to a fallen log next to the ladder. "Can we sit down? I promise I'll explain."

Again they hesitated, but Maggie nodded and took the first step forward. "How did you know we'd be out here?"

Charlie sat on a low rung of the tower ladder, facing them on the log. They shined their lights at an angle so everyone's faces were visible through the darkness. "I left you the message on the boulder next to the river in *Kingdom*."

"*You* sent it?" exclaimed Andrew.

"We thought that was from Bryce," said Jess.

Maggie looked confused. "Did you talk to Bryce?"

Charlie nodded. "Sorry, let me start over. I was recruited for an exclusive programming group by a company called Q2. Have you heard of them?"

"Yeah," replied Andrew. "We've heard of 'em all right."

"Bryce was on my programming team," Charlie continued. "We helped complete the coding sequences for the Eden machine, which, as you likely know if you've talked to

Zach, created a bridge to the virtual world. Things took a bad turn, and when we discovered what they were up to, we tried to block them. But they learned of our plans, and we had to use the Eden machine to escape into the virtual world."

"Then why are you here?" asked Maggie. "How did you get out of *Kingdom*?"

Charlie shook his head. "I never made it into the machine. Someone shot me in the programming room just as things were being activated. Only Bryce and Rachel made it across."

"Rachel?" Maggie repeated, a hint of concern in her voice. "Who's that?"

"She was the third member of our team. She and Bryce crossed the bridge together."

Andrew spoke up. "Hang tight a minute. Zach told us all about what it was like inside *Kingdom* with Bryce. But he didn't say anything about a girl being there."

"Yeah…" Charlie nodded, his eyes dropping to the ground. "Bryce told me she didn't make it. The Rangers gunned her down on the inside."

"Oh my god," whispered Jess.

Charlie looked back at them. "Where is Zach? I was reaching out to him. Why isn't he with you?"

"They took him," said Andrew. "Just yesterday."

Charlie closed his eyes. "Q2?"

"No, actually," said Maggie. "It was some military guys."

"The Chinese military was here?" asked Charlie.

"No, it was our military," explained Jess. "They were

some of General Weber's men. He's taken over most of the JOSHUA project from Professor Hendrickson and my brother. They have Zach in quarantine at Quantico. They're worried he might be infected or something from crossing the bridge and being inside the virtual world."

"Your brother?" said Charlie. "Who's your brother?"

"Tyler Barnes."

Charlie's jaw dropped. "You're Tyler's sister?"

"Try to keep up, man," said Andrew.

"Tell us more about Bryce," said Maggie. "Did you see him? Is he safe? What did he tell you?"

"And how did you talk to him if you're over here and he's over there?" said Andrew. "Also, I thought they shot you?"

Charlie nodded again. "Sorry. I haven't seen him in person, but I've talked to him on the inside. Let me explain —there's a lot to understand. After Bryce and Rachel went across the bridge, the whole place was going to hell in a handbasket, and everybody at Q2 was completely freaking out. Yao was pissed, and he ordered Fitz, the lead programmer, to find Bryce and Rachel, whatever the cost. He dispatched Rangers throughout the game to flush the two of them out.

"They'd shot me in the shoulder, and I was bleeding a ton. One of their goons dragged me back to my room in the compound and just left me to die. I can't explain why I'm still alive, to tell you the truth. The bullet must have missed the important parts. Right after they dumped me in my room, I blacked out. But when I woke up, I was able to bandage the wound and put enough pressure on it to stop the bleeding. Somehow I survived like that for a day or two. When I stumbled out of my room, everybody was gone. It was like the whole operation had just packed up and left."

"What did you do?" asked Jess.

"Yeah, didn't you need to eat something?" said Andrew. "You can only make it three days without food."

"That's water," said Jess.

Andrew frowned. "Whatever. You know what I mean."

"Luckily for me, I could get into the cafeteria where there were still a lot of consumables. Like I said, everyone kind of just disappeared. What they left behind let me lie low while I recovered."

"But wasn't that weeks ago?" asked Andrew. "What have you been doing?"

"And didn't the government shut down that whole compound?" asked Jess.

Charlie nodded. "I found a broken window in an auxiliary building behind the main compound. There was an initial flurry of activity when the Feds came in and locked things down, but that subsided. I had no idea who I could trust or who was watching, so I was scared to go home or contact my grandma back in Edgarton. I didn't want to put my family in any more danger.

"As far as Q2 knew, I was dead, and the Feds didn't know I was there in the first place. I realized that being a ghost isn't such a bad thing if you want to stay off the grid. No one was looking for me, so I could go in and out when I pleased. Eventually I found a way to tap into the mainframe in the central computing lab. That's where I coded an interface and found a connection to Bryce. He was still using one of the functions we'd developed on our team project that we didn't show to Q2. That's likely the only reason they haven't discovered him already. He's hiding out in an underground lab within *Kingdom*."

Maggie's eyes opened wide. "He's underground? Is he safe?"

"I don't think he's hurt," said Charlie. "And for the moment he seems safe. He told me how he'd sent Zach across the bridge using Hendrickson's machine, but that he'd been snagged trying to get back through the portal. Somehow he got away from the Rangers, and he's been on the run ever since."

"We know all about the Rangers," said Andrew. He told Charlie how the Sportsman had come after them in Milton and up at Tech.

Charlie shook his head. "Damn. That's wild."

"Yeah." Andrew nodded at Maggie. "You should have seen her Jeep. He turned it to Swiss cheese."

Maggie wiped her cheek. "What's Bryce doing down in this lab?"

"He's been hiding out," said Charlie. "But things are about to change. He wants to end things."

"End things?" asked Jess. "What do you mean?"

"Q2 scattered after Zach returned across the bridge," Charlie answered. "We think Yao is back in China, likely with his key advisor, a Swedish guy named Sturgis. Fitz is hiding out somewhere with access to the mainframe. The only person we haven't accounted for is Dr. Avanair."

"Heather Avanair?" asked Jess.

Charlie looked surprised. "How did you know her name?"

"They have her locked up," said Andrew, who then explained what they'd learned in Quantico.

"What did she do?" asked Maggie, sounding like she was ready to go another round in the hallway. "For Q2, I mean."

"She was a real trip," said Charlie, shaking his head. "She ran most of the orientation program. She was like our handler, basically. She comes across as all pretty and innocent, but I'm telling you, she's a snake. She's the one who shot me."

"She seemed like a snake from the few minutes that we saw her," agreed Maggie. She stared back at Charlie. "Were she and Bryce... close?"

"I wouldn't say close." Charlie hesitated, but then looked back at Maggie. "Like I said, she had a way of trying to use her womanly wiles on you, but I wouldn't worry. Bryce wasn't having any of it. I think he saw through her act pretty quickly. We were all so worked to the bone with late-night programming assignments, we didn't have time to think about anything else.

"It was crazy stressful. I went over the edge for a while before it all ended. I made some terrible decisions that cost me, that cost us..." His voice cracked and he looked off into the trees. "I tried to make up for it, at least partially.

But I owe him, and Rachel too. That's why I went looking for them. It's why I talked to him, and it's why I'm here meeting with you. Bryce wanted me to help him stop Yao, and he insisted that you all stayed safe."

"I don't know what will happen to Zach," said Andrew quietly. "Those military guys are no joke. They've got nukes, you know."

Jess rolled her eyes. "Don't start that again."

Charlie nodded and asked them to tell him more about how Zach was taken away. He folded his arms and thought for a few moments, then looked up at them with a grin. "Maybe we can get him out."

"Who?" said Maggie. "Zach or Bryce?"

Charlie laughed. "Well, both of them. But first, I was thinking about Zach."

"Dude, weren't you listening?" asked Andrew. "He's locked up. They have him in who knows what kind of prison, psych ward, or wherever they take people to disappear, and he's in the middle of a military base. How do you expect to get him out?"

Charlie turned to Jess. "Do you think your brother knows exactly where Zach's being held?"

She nodded her head. "He could probably find out from Hendrickson. But I don't think he'll agree to break Zach out. He'd get in too much trouble. And they'll have a ton of security. You'd have to be practically invisible."

Charlie grinned. "Like I said, being a ghost has its advantages. You'd be surprised what I can do with a laptop and access to a high-speed network server."

"But what's that going to solve?" asked Maggie. "Even if by some miracle you could get Zach out of quarantine, wouldn't that just bring more people after us? They'd only send him back and probably lock us all up. It would make things worse."

"There's one more thing I haven't told you," said Charlie.

"You have embarrassing pictures of General Weber that we can use to blackmail him?" asked Andrew.

Charlie laughed and stood in front of the ladder. "No, but Bryce has a plan. It's a little crazy, but it just might work."

"What kind of plan?" asked Maggie.

"A way to take the offensive. Bryce wants to turn Q2's efforts against them and open the bridge from the inside to force his way out. Then we have to knock the bridge out of commission. Permanently."

Andrew looked skeptical. "We're going to do all that ourselves?"

Charlie nodded. "We'll need Tyler's help, and probably Hendrickson's too, but it has to happen. The technology is way too dangerous to be left in Yao's hands or even with our own government. We're the only ones who can stop them."

"Bryce said that?" asked Maggie.

Charlie nodded back to her confidently. "He did."

Maggie stood next to him and stared off into the darkness. "Then let's get started."

CHAPTER THIRTEEN

Yao stared at the deep green and purple clusters until the images blurred in his vision. He blinked his eyes and unconsciously stroked the lump on his throat with two bony fingers.

"Are you okay, sir? Would you like to take a break?"

Yao lowered his hand from his throat and turned his attention back to Sturgis. "I am fine. Just thinking."

"Of course, sir." Sturgis shuffled papers in his lap and then slid a different colored graph across the desk. "What are your directions?"

Yao knew the clusters, both the cancerous legions within his deteriorating body and those created by the cosmic tear from the bridge, were growing. Sturgis's report urged the immediate suspension of all work on the new bridge. Suspending the work would mean a lengthy delay in the bridge's activation. And that was unacceptable.

STEVEN K. SMITH

The work must go on. The bridge must be built. There was no room for discussion.

"Construction will continue," Yao announced firmly. "There will be no delays." The bridge's construction on the skyscraper's topmost floor was cloaked under the guise of building an elaborate rooftop swimming pool.

"But sir…" Sturgis proceeded cautiously. "You undoubtedly see the instability in the charts. The tear is growing. If we attempt to activate the machine on schedule as you're suggesting, it's quite possible, likely even, that we'll accelerate the disintegration. It may throw things into permanent imbalance. The implications of what that could mean for the world as we know it, our very existence, could be catastrophic."

Sturgis paused, caught between his fear of the alarming scientific data and the consequences of challenging his superior. "Continuing may not produce the effect that you think it will, sir."

Yao's eyes narrowed. He detested being contradicted by anyone, even a trusted man like Sturgis. "I would warn you not to test my patience, Johannes. That would be a grave miscalculation, despite your tenure. You have your orders. I expect you to execute them, or I will find someone else who will. Are we clear?"

Sturgis nodded quickly. "Very well, sir."

Yao sighed when the man remained in his chair. "Is there something more?"

Sturgis swallowed hard. "Two things, I'm afraid."

Yao twirled his finger impatiently. "Continue, then."

"Our sources back in the States report that Ms. Avanair was captured by the American government. They've taken her into custody for questioning and are holding her at Quantico. It's unclear if they know exactly who they have, since per your protocol, she'd be traveling under a solid alias."

Yao waved his hand. "If they took her to Quantico, then they know who they have. Or at least a strong suspicion."

"It's very likely, sir. What would you like to do?"

Yao thought quietly for a moment. "Send a message to our friend, Mr. Cox. Explain the sensitivity of the situation. We'll pay double his normal rate, but he needs to take care of it immediately."

Sturgis looked back in surprise. "Are you sure, sir? I mean, Dr. Avanair is highly trained in resisting—"

Yao lifted a lone finger. "You said there were two items?"

Sturgis glanced at his briefing folder. "The last piece is an update from Mr. Fitz. He remains on schedule with their final sequencing. The activation program should be completed in concert with the portal construction on the roof."

"Excellent."

Sturgis hesitated. "One related item, sir. Security logs from our gaming division indicate that an external entity has breached a sensitive area within the virtual dimension. While it's unclear how he arrived there, we suspect it may be our rogue recruit, Bryce Pearson."

"What kind of sensitive area?" asked Yao.

"An inner control lab that could provide access into the

mainframe. However, Mr. Fitz assures me that his firewalls are impenetrable, and it should be no cause for concern."

"Of course he does." Yao slapped the desktop with his palm. Bringing the adolescent recruits into the programming teams was one of his few regrets. The benefits of the low-cost workforce were negated by their idealism and unpredictability. It was time to clean up loose ends. The foolishness with young Bryce would stop now.

"I've had enough of that annoying mosquito buzzing in my ear. Send in some Rangers to finish the job they should have already completed in the first place."

"Very well, sir." Sturgis stood, bowed quickly, and exited the room.

Yao swiveled his chair and stared at the city's glimmering lights scattered across the dark view. It was time to move things to completion. The final sequence must be activated. He knew from the growing sensations inside his body that his expiration date was close. If they didn't complete the new machine and move the bridge to full operation, he would be stuck here, destined to an unknown eternity beyond his control. That was one development he refused to allow, the threat of cosmic instability be damned.

CHAPTER FOURTEEN

Zach stared across the white-walled room. The metal bed frame, thin white sheets over the mattress, small table and chair, and bathroom were all very bland and antiseptic. They had taken him to a building near the FBI's headquarters at Quantico and put him in a wing shared with a hospital for veterans suffering from PTSD. But the small space seemed more like a cell than a hospital room.

A simple meal and a glass of water had been on the table when he arrived. He'd hesitated to try either at first, wondering if they had been poisoned, but his hunger got the best of him and he finished both quickly. As far as he could tell, it was just normal food and drink.

When he'd arrived, they'd run him through a process like pictures he'd seen of immigrants arriving at Ellis Island by the Statue of Liberty. Military nurses took his temperature, blood pressure, height and weight, and then they attached some sensors to his chest, head, and places he didn't want to think about, to get readings from every millimeter of his body, inside and out. He was poked and prodded like a science experiment, just like Professor Hendrickson had warned.

None of it hurt, really, or at least not most of it. They'd shaved his hair into a buzz cut like General Weber's. Zach figured it was so they could see his hair grow without the coloring, but it felt weird, short and stiff like a brush. He felt like he'd just been drafted into Army basic training. The only time he'd had such short hair was once in the second grade when his whole class got lice. His mom had chopped it off then, claiming it would be easier to care for, but he hadn't liked it, and he'd kept it longer ever since.

They'd also made him change out of his clothes, giving him only a thin hospital gown to wear over his underwear. The room temperature was comfortable, but he felt ridiculous and self-conscious when any of the doctors or nurses came in.

Perhaps the worst part was that no one would speak to him except to give instructions for the next test. They ignored his questions and his pleas to see his parents. God, he tried not to imagine what his mom and dad must be feeling. The past few months had been like a nightmare with Bryce's disappearance. He'd wanted to tell them the truth a hundred times, but he could never go through with it.

And now he'd been dragged away from the house like a criminal. Did the government give them an explanation? Had they cooked up some story that he'd been exposed to a dangerous disease and quarantined? Or did they say that he'd committed a crime? There was no use guessing, and it was easier not to think about it.

The door lock beeped and a man in a white lab coat entered the room. Zach jerked up in his bed and stared. The man was about Zach's dad's age, with round glasses and longer hair than the rest of the military people he'd seen. In fact, under the lab coat, he wore a regular white dress shirt with a yellow tie and navy dress pants.

"Hello, Zach. How are you holding up?" The man spoke like the pediatrician at Zach's annual checkup. He smiled warmly, although he didn't reach out his hand to shake Zach's, or say what his name was. He pulled the chair from the table and sat facing Zach on the bed.

"Oh, just great," Zach answered. "Other than being stuck in here like a prisoner. When are you letting me out?" What did they think he would do, thank them for the free meal and a quiet place to rest?

"I'm sorry for the inconvenience, Zach. Are you comfortable?"

He tugged at the bottom of the gown, making sure it covered his knees. "You mean besides having to wear this dress?"

"I'm afraid that is necessary until we complete our initial testing phase."

Zach rolled his eyes. Not more tests.

"But I promise that you're in the care of some of the very best doctors," the man said.

"Yeah, whatever. I thought this was a free country. You

always lock people up like this when they didn't do anything wrong?"

The man ignored the question. "Zach, do you know why you're here?"

He let out a long breath and tried to calm down. Yelling wouldn't help anything. He'd already tried that, and he was still here. Maybe if he just answered this guy's questions, they'd be done with him and let him go. There was no point hiding things. They clearly knew what had happened. He just had to show them he was fine.

"Probably because you found out about my crossing the bridge and being with Bryce inside *Kingdom*," Zach answered. He noticed for the first time a clear, tiny earpiece tucked inside the man's left ear. Was he being instructed by someone else? Were they also listening to his responses?

The man studied his notes and then looked back at him. "Why didn't you tell General Weber that you'd entered the JOSHUA machine?"

"Nobody asked me."

"Did someone tell you to keep it a secret?"

Zach thought about the best way to answer that. He didn't want to throw Hendrickson and Tyler under the bus. He knew they'd been trying to help. But they *had* said to keep it to himself. "Not in so many words," Zach answered.

The man wrote something on his chart. "But someone made it clear that it would be better if you didn't tell. Is that right?"

"I guess."

"Why do you think that is, Zach?"

"Beats me."

The man raised an eyebrow. "If you had to guess."

"Um... well, maybe they thought all this would happen."

"This?"

"Yeah, this." Zach waved his arm at the room. He felt his anger returning. "Me getting locked up and grilled like I was a terrorist or something. What's next, are you going to ship me off to Guantanamo? I have rights. I didn't get a phone call. I want to talk to a lawyer."

"You're not under arrest," the man answered softly.

"Then why won't you let me out?"

"It's for your own safety," said the man. "And the safety of those around you."

Zach froze. He hadn't considered that they might have taken the others. Were Andrew, Jess, or Maggie there in quarantine too?

"Can you describe for us what you saw going across the bridge in the JOSHUA machine?" the man asked. "Take your time, and try to be as specific as possible."

Zach sighed and flashed back to when he'd stepped into the machine. It was something he thought about often. It was hard to forget. The man jotted a lot of notes in his pad as Zach described the experience of stepping into the green mist of the chamber, the forces pressing against him, and flying across the tunnel of light until he splashed down into the canyon pool.

"What did you do once you were in *Kingdom*?" the man asked after Zach had finished. Zach recounted how Bryce had found him, their journey across the Central Plateau, and their struggle at the return portal at the chasm.

The man turned from his pad and looked straight in Zach's eyes. "But as far as you know, your brother is still there? Inside the virtual world?"

"That's right."

"Was there anyone else there with you? Besides your brother?"

Zach shook his head. "Not unless you count the Rangers or those night cats that attacked us by the chasm. We heard some virtual game players in the distance, but we never saw anyone up close. We were the only real people, if that's what you mean."

"Yes, thank you. We're almost done." He glanced at his notes. "How do you feel now, Zach?"

Zach shook his head. This was stupid. "Just awesome, thanks. I love being a human guinea pig. How about you?"

The man ignored his remark but continued with the questions. "Why did you dye your hair?"

"I didn't want my parents to worry..." He struggled to push back the tears welling up in his eyes. He took a deep breath. "I didn't want them to worry," he repeated, and left it at that. He was all done answering. It was time for him to ask some questions. "How long am I going to be in here?"

"I can't give you a firm answer on that right now, Zach," said the man. "But I promise we're doing everything we can."

He sounded just like General Weber. "Can I see my

parents? Or can I at least talk to them? Call them on the phone?"

There was another silence, like the man was listening to outside opinions through his earpiece. "I'll see what I can do, Zach."

"Does Professor Hendrickson know that I'm in here? Maybe he can help you understand that there's nothing to worry about. I've been back from *Kingdom* for weeks. Nothing's happened. I feel totally fine. If you'll just listen to what I'm saying, you'll understand that—"

The man abruptly stood. "That's all for now, Zach. Thank you for your responses. We will bring you another meal in a little while. Get some rest."

CHAPTER FIFTEEN_

Tyler carried the last of the patio chairs into the back of the garage. He turned and faced his sister, who'd been stalking him around the yard ever since she got off the bus that afternoon. "Forget it, Jess, it's not happening."

Jess shook her head stubbornly. "Why not?"

"All kinds of reasons."

"Such as?"

Tyler rolled his eyes and plopped into a chair. "First, Hendrickson will have my head if I go around him and give you that information."

"He'll get over it," Jess replied.

"Right. Easy for you to say. Second, the government is up all of our asses over this. They're the ones who locked Zach up in the first place. What do you think they'll say if we sneak him out of there? General Weber will throw us in the brig and throw away the key."

"The brig?" Jess scoffed and shook her head. "What are you, in the Navy now? They wouldn't do that."

"Trust me. I'm as replaceable as anyone else. I don't think you realize how torqued up the military is over this. They think in worst-case scenarios."

"Like what?"

"Like World War III, that's what. They don't want someone like Yao having control over cross-dimensional transport. Plus, I told you before, there's something going on since the bridge was activated. They're worried the strange readings might lead to something worse."

"Such as?"

"Such as the universe imploding. Cataclysmic failure across the cosmos. Bad stuff. They don't even know what to be afraid of. This is all tapping into the complete unknown, Jess. It may have started out for you guys as playing a video game, but it's way, way bigger than that now. I'm worried about Zach and Bryce too, but we have to be smart."

Jess kicked an empty water bottle across the garage floor. "So what are you even doing here, Ty? You've barely been home for what, like, three years, and now you just pop in to say hi, and to move patio furniture? Why bother if you're not even going to help us?"

Tyler shook his head. "I know I haven't stayed as close as I should have. That's my bad, and I want to do better. But I'm worried about you. Whether you knew it or not, I've been busy working on this project for months with Hendrickson. I've studied the science, and I even helped program much of the interface for JOSHUA. I wasn't kidding when I told you I was in line to test things out."

"Why didn't you tell us?" asked Jess. "Why keep it all a secret? You even lied to us about your major!"

"Because it's a dangerous business, Jess. I wanted to protect you. I didn't want you in the middle of it."

"It's too late for that. Don't be naïve yourself, Tyler. We're already in the middle, like it or not."

"Well, then I don't want it to get worse."

"Ty…" said Jess. "We can't just leave Bryce over there. I promised Maggie. I promised Zach that we'd help. You should see the boys' parents. Imagine what Mom and Dad would do if you'd gone missing like Bryce, and then suddenly I was locked up in a government quarantine. Wouldn't you do everything you could to get me out, to help our family?"

Tyler sighed. "Sure, but—"

She waved him off. "Let me finish. I'm not a little kid anymore. I understand that you've been plugged into this longer than I have, and I agree that you know much more about what could go wrong and how it works than the rest of us. But that's exactly why we need you. I don't think it's a coincidence that when we all got stuck in this with Zach, you just happened to be the person who was working with Hendrickson. Do you? I mean, god, I'm your sister, and I didn't have a clue what you were doing. But you were the only one who could help then, and you're the only one who can help get Charlie access to reach Zach now."

Tyler stood and paced around the garage. "I don't know

what you think is going to happen. I mean, say we somehow get into the government compound, find where they have Zach locked up, open his door—which is surely locked down tight, get him to come with you, and then make it out of the building without being seen. They'd still just come take him right back."

"That's what we told Charlie," said Jess, nodding.

Tyler frowned. "Oh, and don't forget that the entire place is secured by the United States military. Am I missing anything?"

"No, I think you covered it."

"Right. So after all that, what's the point? It still won't help Bryce. General Weber is going to do what he's going to do, and there isn't a damn thing we can do about it."

Jess bit her lip, but then she smiled. "Unless we have a plan."

Tyler stared back at her. "*Do* you have a plan?"

"Bryce does."

CHAPTER SIXTEEN

"Okay, let's go over the next part." Charlie stood next to the whiteboard which held the diagrams of the plan. They'd set up a makeshift planning center in the room above Jess and Tyler's garage.

"Dude, I'm starving. You said we'd be done by dinner," Andrew moaned. "That was an hour ago. Where's the food?"

Maggie shushed him. "Don't you want to help Zach?"

"Of course I do. But at this rate, the rest of us will also have white hair by the time we see him."

"Just zip it then." Jess opened a drawer and tossed Andrew a small bag of pretzels. She nodded for Charlie to start again.

Charlie started at the far left. "Tyler will drive to the government building with me hiding in the trunk. He'll use Hendrickson's clearance codes to gain access to the parking garage. When we're safely in the garage, I'll sneak out and take the service elevator up to the fifth floor."

"And you're sure that elevator won't be locked?" asked Maggie.

Charlie nodded. "Already taken care of. I found the maintenance interface on the government server." He held up a small device with wires connected to a plastic swipe card. "This temporary patch card will operate the elevator door. By the time their security flags the breach, we'll be long gone."

"And if it happens faster than you think?" said Andrew.

Charlie grinned. "Then we'll have to boogie. But it won't happen. I've done this before."

Andrew's eyebrows raised. "You've broken into a government facility?"

"Well, local government. It was the county records office back in Edgarton. I needed a slight adjustment to my economics midterm grade sophomore year, but it's all the same thing."

Andrew chuckled. "Sure it is."

"Okay," Tyler interrupted, glancing at the time on his phone. "Keep going. Our parents will be back in an hour, and I want to make sure all this is away."

"I thought you'd moved out?" asked Andrew.

Tyler shrugged. "I have, but somehow when I come back, I'm back under their rules. It's annoying."

Jess gave him a look. "So that's why you never come back…"

Tyler winced. "Anyway… so once Charlie takes the elevator to the fifth floor, I'll monitor the building security cameras on my laptop from the garage." He handed Charlie a small earpiece. "You'll be able to hear me through this. I'll help guide you through the halls to Zach's room and keep you from running into trouble."

"Wouldn't it just be easier to take out their cameras altogether?" asked Jess. "I mean, that way they wouldn't see you at all."

"Despite what you see in the movies, that's harder than it seems," Tyler answered. "And if we knock out their whole system, they'll be on high alert, which means they will tighten security even more. That would stop the elevators and lock down the exits, and we'd all be screwed."

Maggie looked back at the board. "Okay, so you're guiding Charlie through the halls. He evades the guards, and makes it to the room where they're holding Zach. Then what?"

"I expect their interior door lock codes will be on a higher level than the elevators, so given what we know about their basic security interface, I've rigged this decoder." Charlie held up a small electronic device slightly bigger than his cell phone. "It plugs into the circuit board on the door panel, identifies the lock frequency, and then opens the door."

"Where'd you try that one?" said Andrew, skeptically. "The public library?"

"I gave it to him," said Tyler. "Hendrickson developed it

during the construction of the JOSHUA machine. It works. Trust me."

Andrew shook his head. "It better."

"So I'll slip into Zach's room," continued Charlie, "and quickly explain what's happening. Then we'll retrace our steps along the halls, take the maintenance elevator back to the garage, hop into Tyler's car, and jet out of there."

"And what happens then, exactly?" asked Maggie, hesitantly. "Won't they immediately come and haul him back?"

"That was my concern too," agreed Tyler. He stepped over to a laptop on the desk. "But Charlie shared some insights that won me over."

"He did?" asked Andrew.

"Well, Charlie and someone else important." Tyler punched a few more keystrokes on the computer, and the wall monitor next to the whiteboard came to life. A flickering image in the outline of a face filled the screen.

Maggie gasped. "Oh, my god…"

"Is that who I think it is?" asked Andrew, leaning forward.

Tyler grinned as the face became clearer.

"Bryce!" Maggie leaped up next to the screen.

"As soon as I activate the microphone on the webcam, we can talk to each other," explained Tyler. He tapped a few more keys. "There, it should work now."

"Bryce, it's Maggie. Can you see me?" She looked like she was about to lift off the ground from excitement. Bryce's face was unresponsive for a few long seconds, but then he smiled, and his lips started moving.

"Hey, Mags. Where've you been hiding?"

The voice was distorted, but it was him. Maggie covered her mouth and tears streamed down her cheeks. She wiped her face and inched closer to the screen. "Are you okay? I've missed you so much."

There was another delay, but then Bryce nodded, turning his head gently to the side. "I'm making it, babe. I'm so sorry that all this has happened. I never meant to leave you."

Maggie's voice came out in forced breaths. "I know. It's okay. We're all so worried about you. I just want you to come home."

Bryce's hand pointed out toward her. "You still have it."

Maggie looked down and realized she was holding her necklace in her fingers. She laughed softly. "Promise me you'll get back, Bryce. I need to hear you say it."

He lowered his glance away from the monitor and stared right at her. "I promise, Mags."

No one wanted to interrupt the moment, but finally Tyler signaled to Charlie that they had to keep going. "Bryce, I'm glad you're still safe," Charlie called. "Is everything coming along on your end?"

Bryce nodded, his words slightly out of sync with his mouth. "It's going to take more work, but the sequencing is coming along—" The screen flickered. Bryce's face disappeared for a couple seconds and then bounced back. The sound was interrupted, and most of the words came out garbled.

Maggie turned into the room. "Is he okay?"

114

"I think we're losing the connection," Tyler answered.

"It's the relay," said Charlie. "It's a delicate routing I rigged up to port our feed across the back channels of the game interface. You never know how long it'll last."

The image of Bryce's face moved for a few more seconds, flickered, and then disappeared. They sat quietly in the room staring at the blank screen.

"It was really him," Maggie muttered. She turned to Charlie and Tyler, another tear slipping down her cheek. "Thank you for that."

Charlie nodded. "I told you. I promised that I'd help him."

"So what's he working on over there?" asked Andrew.

"He's found a virtual reproduction of the main programming room from Q2's headquarters," said Charlie. "It's where Bryce, Rachel, and I were working for Fitz. It's a lot like the cavern you described with the JOSHUA machine, but this one has Q2's mainframe and the Eden machine."

"But it's not real?" asked Jess.

Charlie shrugged. "It's hard to say…"

"'Real' is relative in this context," said Tyler. "We think it's a programmed recreation of the Q2 lab. The image of Fitz is just a hologram, but it also has actual computers with a working mainframe interface into both the game and Q2's servers."

"Bryce and I could see that Fitz is working on activating a new transmission device," said Charlie. "He's hiding out remotely, and from the looks of it, he's nearly finished with a whole new strand of execution sequences. We think they're designed to allow Yao to unlock the power of the bridge from multiple locations, independent of dedicated machines like Eden or JOSHUA."

"You mean they're going to open the bridge?" asked Andrew.

"We think so," said Tyler.

"Didn't General Weber say Yao is back in China?" asked Jess.

"Probably," Tyler answered. "But he can now try to open the bridge from anywhere. We're not sure why, but he seems to be intent on making that happen quickly."

"So can Bryce use their bridge to get home?" asked Maggie.

"That's our hope," answered Tyler, "but as I explained to Jess, there's a boatload of risks that we know nothing about. Things could easily go haywire and quickly spiral out of our control."

"As long as there's a chance," Maggie whispered, rolling the necklace chain through her fingers.

Jess rested her arm around Maggie's shoulder. "We're trying."

"So what's Bryce working on?" asked Andrew. "He can't be trying to stop Fitz's plans, or else he won't be able to use the bridge to get home. Will he have to go to China?"

"What he is doing is more of a hack than a stop," answered Charlie. "Like Tyler said, the new programming would allow the bridge to transmit from multiple locations. Yao will likely be opening it from Shanghai, but if we can leverage the same code to let us open it here, or close to Milton, Bryce can cross it to get back home."

Jess tried to imagine the bridge opening into Milton. "That sounds dangerous."

"It's all dangerous," answered Tyler. "That's why General Weber is so worried about it. It's only a matter of time until the military moves to shut things down permanently."

"We have to get Bryce back before that happens," said Maggie.

Charlie nodded. "Exactly."

Andrew glanced at the door. "But first, we have to rescue Zach."

"That's right," replied Tyler. "So, go home and get a good night's sleep. Charlie and I leave for Quantico first thing in the morning. The rest of you act normally, but be ready for Maggie to pick you up at school."

"At the end of third period," said Maggie. "Don't go through the office. I'll meet you in the side parking lot between the middle school and the high school."

Andrew groaned. "I have gym third period."

Jess smacked his arm. "Deal with it."

"You all need to be clear of Milton and on your way to the meeting point up the mountain by the time we leave the government building with Zach," said Tyler. "Once they realize he's gone, they'll be looking for us all." He paused and glanced at each of their faces. "Once we start this, there's no turning back."

"It started a long time ago," said Maggie. "We have to rescue them both. There's no other choice."

"Are we good?" asked Tyler.

"Good." Jess nodded.

"I'm in," said Andrew.

Charlie ran his fingers through his shaggy red hair and smiled wide. "Rock on."

CHAPTER SEVENTEEN_

I t was dark in the car's trunk except for a red glow from the brake lights whenever Tyler stopped at a traffic signal. Charlie glanced at the time on his watch. They should be there any minute. If they could just get inside the building, he felt confident he'd be able to make it from there. But if a guard at the entrance searched the trunk, he wasn't sure how he'd explain his hiding spot. He hoped it wouldn't come to that. This was a risk worth taking.

He'd already experienced captivity in a compound like this. Q2 wasn't much different from the government, the way he saw it—slightly different motivations, perhaps, but the same result. Both groups were more concerned about their plans than their impact on individual rights. If a single person had to rot in a cell for days or years to maintain what "they" saw as the greater good, so be it.

Charlie couldn't let that happen. It had been years since

he'd visited his deadbeat dad in the joint, but it had left a lasting image in his mind. He wasn't going to let Bryce's little brother face that same future. Charlie's father had brought his fate on himself, but Zach had just been in the wrong place at the wrong time.

"Here we go." Tyler's voice filled Charlie's head through the earpiece. Ironically, Charlie had swiped most of this equipment from the tech storage depot at Q2's building. He smiled, thinking of how pissed Yao would be if he knew he'd helped supply their resistance.

The vehicle rocked to a stop. Charlie heard a voice speaking to Tyler up at the driver's side window. Footsteps on the pavement circled the car. They paused right outside the trunk. Charlie made like a statue, holding his breath, as if a simple exhale would give him away. Were they about to open the trunk or were they simply inspecting the undercarriage? It seemed like forever, but finally the guard spoke again and the car inched forward.

"We're in," said Tyler. They drove to the bottom floor of the three-level underground parking garage beneath the government building. If it had been the main Quantico complex, their task would have been much harder, but the information Tyler had acquired showed that Zach was being held in a side building that was part of the VA hospital. It had a lower level of security. Charlie had found Zach's name on the patient room logs. Then he'd pulled the building plans from the county commissioner's office under the Freedom of Information Act. They'd shown the bottom parking level as the easiest access point to the service elevator.

The engine turned off. Charlie heard Tyler's door close before he walked around to open the trunk. The trunk lid cracked. Charlie's body unfolded from the tight space, like Dracula emerging from a coffin.

"That was close," he said to Tyler as he stretched his legs. "I thought they were about to find me."

"I thought so too." Tyler reached in to retrieve his equipment bag that Charlie had been using as a headrest inside the trunk. "You ready?"

Charlie nodded. "Let's do it."

Tyler sat back in the driver's seat and opened up his laptop next to him on the armrest. "I'll be with you the whole way," he said through the open door. "Just go slow. If you run into trouble, remember those supply closets we identified in the floor plans. They're your best spots to hide until it's clear." He glanced at his screen and pointed to the right. "The service elevator should be over in that corner." He reached out and gave Charlie a quick fist-bump. "Good luck."

"You too," Charlie said, as he pulled on a backpack holding his supplies. The garage was only half-full, and so far, all the people seemed to be inside at work. He knew there were likely security cameras, but he walked casually and hoped he'd just blend in. He'd borrowed one of Tyler's suits to better look the part, but he felt constricted and self-consciously tugged at the top button of his collar.

The last time he'd worn a tie was for his dad's court sentencing, just before they'd sent him away. The lawyer had told them that dressing up would make a better impression with the judge, but it didn't matter. That was nearly six years ago, but he'd sworn he'd never wear a tie again. He glanced down at the blue material hanging down the front of his shirt and shook his head. He'd never imagined being in a situation like this, but he still didn't like it.

Most of the time he tried not to think about his old man, but it was hard not to. Living dirt poor in the sticks outside Edgarton wasn't the life he wanted. If his mom could have seen how he'd been living with his grandma and cousins, she'd probably have rolled over in her grave. Charlie had sworn he'd get out as soon as he could. California, maybe. The farther away the better.

He pulled out the override card he'd programmed and swiped it across the square sensor. "Open sesame," he muttered as a green light quickly illuminated, and the elevator door slid to the right. Charlie stepped inside, scanning the parking garage for movement as the doors closed, but all seemed quiet.

"Heading up to the fifth floor," he said into the mic on his wrist. He and Tyler had agreed to share brief location updates on a private frequency, but the less they spoke the better. Security might still monitor the airwaves, and it would look suspicious if he was chattering into his wrist as he walked the halls.

Charlie played through his route in his mind as the elevator ascended. The fifth floor was actually eight levels up, since they were on the lowest of the three parking decks. He tensed as they passed each floor because of the chance that someone else might call for the service elevator. When the LED panel flashed "5," Charlie tugged the strap of his backpack, brushed his hair over his ears, and readied himself as the door opened.

He stepped out into a generic white-walled hallway. The usual sounds of an office building floated through the air all around him. He followed the floor plan in his head, turning right out of the elevator and going down the hall. The fake ID badge that Tyler had helped him construct hung from his belt. He walked purposefully but calmly, like he was an IT guy who monitored the network servers and was just doing his job. He figured he could talk his way out of things if anyone questioned him.

"There are two people walking toward you around the next corner," warned Tyler's voice from the garage. Charlie jumped, having nearly forgotten the earpiece. He tried to look relaxed as he turned the corner. A man and woman walked right by him engaged in a deep conversation. They never even looked his way as they passed him.

He made two lefts, then a quick right. Room numbers were printed beside each door. If Tyler's intel from Hendrickson's office was correct, Zach's room should be just ahead on the left. If they'd moved him to another room, or if Tyler's information was wrong, Charlie would have no choice but to bail. He'd never be able to discretely find Zach in that maze of rooms.

He slid off his backpack as he approached Zach's room

and pulled out the descrambler device. "I'm at the door," he whispered into his wrist before he pulled the front panel off the security box. He attached two silver clips from his device onto the security box's electrical wires and initiated the decoder. A flurry of numbers flew across the screen as the device scanned for the code to crack the door lock. It was an eight-digit code, more complicated than Charlie'd expected, but still doable. It would just take a little longer. Most locks he'd seen were five, six at the most.

He was still three numbers away when Tyler's voice barked in his ear. "We may have a problem. There's a group of people coming your way. I think they might turn onto your hall. You need to fly to the safety zone now or they'll see you. You have five seconds."

Charlie stared at the decoder. Still two numbers away. He cursed as he unhooked the wires and pushed the panel cover tight against the wall. It wouldn't stand up to close inspection, but someone walking past shouldn't notice. He sprinted two doors up on the other side of the hall. He slipped into a supply closet, closing the door just as voices came around the corner. He'd have been toast if he were still standing at the doorway, trying to hack the lock.

The closet was dark, but the door was thin enough that he could hear sounds from the hallway. "Don't move." Tyler said. "They're right outside your door."

The group seemed to have stopped in the hall. What were they doing? He prayed they weren't getting supplies. He strained to listen through the door.

"What's the status of the kid?" a deep voice asked.

"Most of the tests were normal, sir," a woman answered. "Two were inconclusive, however, so we're running them again. He seems to have an elevated heart rate and an abnormal electrical pulse throughout his central nervous system. We've never seen anything like that before. It might explain the discoloration in his hair follicles."

"We're still getting phone calls, General," another man's voice added. "His parents have contacted Senator McMillan's office and they're threatening to go to the press if we don't let them see their son."

"That's the last thing we need," the deep-voiced man replied. Charlie wondered if it was General Weber. "Don't they know what national security means? Goddamn McMillan couldn't find his way out of a paper bag if it didn't have a vote tied to it for his next election. Keep stalling. We need the rest of those tests. Besides, if Hendrickson's data is right, we might have much bigger things to worry about than this kid. What's the status of the woman?"

"Still not talking," replied the other man's voice. "She seems trained in counter interrogation techniques. We're searching the databases to see if she might have worked with the Australian Special Forces."

"Keep at it," the general barked. "She'll crack, eventually. They always do."

They kept talking, but the sound seemed to move further down the hallway and their voices faded. Charlie waited silently in the supply closet until Tyler's voice returned.

"All clear, but be fast."

Charlie snuck back to Zach's door. He reattached the decoder device to the wiring. The final two numbers came through quickly, and when the door lock clicked open, he replaced the scanner panel and slipped inside.

CHAPTER EIGHTEEN_

Zach had been locked up for two days, three at the most, and it was wearing on him. He wondered if this was what one of Andrew's nuclear doomsday scenarios would be like. If a bomb dropped, the nuclear fallout could send everyone to underground bunkers without modern-day conveniences. Would they be able to survive after being used to so much technology? Zach's current confinement wasn't quite the same, but every minute he spent alone in the plain, vanilla space, he felt a little closer to the edge of insanity.

He'd met with the doctors at least a dozen times. He never knew if he was passing or failing their never-ending barrage of questions and tests. He felt good, other than the pulses that occasionally ran through his leg, and the color of his hair, of course, but who really knew what was going on inside his body? Maybe crossing dimensions really had messed him up. There could be a tumor or terrible growth beneath his skin that was secretly ravaging his organs.

Maybe he really was dangerous and needed to be locked away from the rest of the population forever for their protection. What kind of life would that be? Would he ever be able to see his family or his friends again? What about school? As much as he liked to complain about Mrs. Craig, he'd gladly exchange Algebra class for being locked up in here.

With so much time on his hands, Zach thought about Bryce often. While Zach had only been inside *Kingdom* for one night, his brother had spent weeks there. Bryce told him that time didn't travel at the same speed on the inside as it did in reality. How long would he feel like he'd been gone? What if it had been years? Did he age like normal within the game, or was he the same, just spinning through eternity, locked far away from all that was familiar and real?

Zach rolled over in the bed and closed his eyes. Thinking about those things only made the hurt worse. He spent most of his time in a series of interrupted sleep and wakefulness.

Zach jerked to alertness at the click of the lock. His body instinctively tensed, preparing for another round of pokes and prods. The motion-sensor lights flipped on as the door opened, gradually brightening the room. He leaned forward in his bed and squinted at the new man standing inside the door. His gray suit and tie fit in with the government agents that roamed the halls, but he looked out of place. His red hair was shaggier than the standard government employee, and he was too young. He looked older than Zach, but he could have easily been Bryce or Maggie's age.

"Zach?" the guy asked quietly, slipping something into a backpack.

Zach swung his feet down to the floor. Nothing really surprised him anymore, but something was off with this guy. "Who are you?"

"My name's Charlie. I'm getting you out of here." He waved Zach over to the doorway.

"Getting me out of here? Who are you?"

The guy named Charlie paused and took a breath. "I'm a friend of Bryce's. He sent me."

Zach sprang to his feet. "Bryce is here?"

Charlie shook his head. "No, he's not here, but I'm working with Tyler and Maggie and your friends. We're breaking you out of here, but we have to hurry."

Zach pulled self-consciously at his hospital gown. He stared at his bare feet. "You want me to go like this?"

Charlie frowned back at him. "Don't you have clothes?"

"They took them. You didn't bring any?"

Charlie groaned. "No, we didn't think of that. Sorry." He opened the door a crack and peeked into the hallway.

"Hang on a second." Zach's knees felt wobbly. "You mean, you don't have any release paperwork? How do you expect to get me out? This place is crawling with military people."

Charlie closed the door and turned back around. "We have a plan, but you'll have to trust me, okay? I promised your brother I'd get you to safety, and I'm not letting him down. But we have to leave now, or we're both going to be jacked."

Zach tried to think of an alternative, but he couldn't. He felt absurd walking down the hallway in his flimsy gown and nothing but his underwear, but he wanted out of this place. If this guy really was working with Bryce and the others, he might be his only hope.

Zach sighed and walked to the door. Charlie held his arm up to his face and spoke into his wrist. "I have the package. Entering the hallway now."

"Who are you talking to?" asked Zach.

"Tyler's in the parking garage. He's monitoring the security cameras." He waved his hand forward. "Come on, and be quiet."

Charlie seemed to know where he was going as they slinked through the hallways. Zach's bare feet felt cold on the tile floor. The hallway wasn't as warm as his room, but adrenaline rushed through his body, keeping him from feeling cold. Charlie stopped short at the next turn and held his hand up. He seemed to be listening to instructions that must be coming from Tyler. Charlie nodded and then pulled Zach by the arm through the closest door and into a stairwell.

"What's wrong?" Zach whispered.

"Someone's coming down the hall. I could pass unnoticed, but you're a little conspicuous in that gown."

"Maybe if you'd brought me some clothes—"

Charlie put his finger to his lips as voices passed by the

stairwell. They both pressed against the wall until it was quiet again. Charlie cursed at something Tyler must have told him through the earpiece. He leaned over the stairwell railing and then turned back to Zach. "Someone's using the service elevator."

"So?"

"That was our exit," Charlie answered. "We'll have to take the stairs. Come on."

"How far are we going?" Zach asked as they tiptoed down the winding metal staircase.

"To the bottom. Lower level of the garage."

As they approached the fourth floor, a door banged below them. They froze and listened. Someone was entering the stairwell.

Charlie pointed at the door, and they scrambled into a fourth-floor hallway. More voices could be heard approaching, so they ducked around the nearest corner. Zach wasn't sure if Tyler was still guiding them, but Charlie suddenly opened another door and shoved Zach through in front of him. It was pitch black with the door closed, but Zach had glimpsed a janitor's closet when the door had first opened.

Charlie unzipped his backpack and pulled out a flashlight and a small map. Zach started to ask a question, but Charlie flipped off the light and covered Zach's mouth as voices passed by in the hall. When it was quiet again, Charlie gently opened the door. He nodded back at Zach and they moved left up the hallway. "Stay close."

Zach thought the stairwell was the other direction, but he kept his mouth shut since he didn't have the earpiece or the map. Charlie was staring at the room numbers along the wall. He stopped at a door and pulled an electronic device from his backpack.

"What are you doing?" Zach hissed, glancing back and forth. "I thought we had to get out of here?"

Charlie nodded. "We do."

"Then why are you stopping?"

Charlie had pulled off the door lock's cover and was connecting some kind of scanner device to the wires. It was probably how he'd opened Zach's door, but why was he doing it again now? The door didn't look like an exit or another elevator. They didn't have time for this.

"It'll just take a second," Charlie muttered, as a flood of numbers shot across the device. "I know what I'm doing."

Zach couldn't tell if Charlie was speaking to him or to Tyler over the radio. What was he doing? The numbers on the scanner turned green and the door lock unlatched. Charlie shot him a serious look just before he opened the door. "Just follow my lead."

CHAPTER NINETEEN

Zach followed Charlie into a room that looked just like the one he'd been held in. Except this one had a woman in it. She sat at a small table, eating lunch. When she glanced up at them, her face filled with surprise.

"Chaalee…" she said, like she'd seen a ghost. "You're alive."

Zach had recognized her even before he'd heard the accent. It was the woman from Q2 that they'd seen in the hallway—Heather Avanair. He pulled at his gown, self-conscious again.

"You don't look too happy to see me," Charlie answered.

"Surprised would be a better word, perhaps. To what do I owe this unexpected visit?" She calmly picked up a piece of pineapple from her plate, put it in her mouth, and then looked back at them.

"Believe it or not, we're getting you out of here," said Charlie.

"We're what?" Zach's head whipped around. "Are you crazy? We need to get out of here before they find us."

Even Heather Avanair looked surprised. "And why would you do that, Chaalee? Did you miss me that much?"

"Don't flatter yourself. Let's just say we're in a unique position to help each other. I get you out of here, and you give me the information I need to get Bryce across the bridge."

Heather glanced at Zach, her eyes narrowed. "Still chasing that brother of yours, are you? It was so nice to finally lay eyes on you the other day, Zach. I hope Maggie's not still sore about what I said." She paused, took another bite, and then stared at him. "Do you think you can trust me to get your brother out?"

Zach didn't know what to say. This was all out of left field.

Heather shook her head before he could answer. "Thanks for the sweet offer, Chaalee, but I think I'll be better off working the Feds than getting caught with you two amateurs. It was so nice to see you, though. You too, Zach. Good luck getting out of here in one piece."

"It's not an option." Charlie suddenly pulled a small handgun from the backpack. "Let's go. Now."

Zach's eyes bulged. He stared at the weapon and then up at Charlie. "Where did you get that?"

Charlie shook him off and turned back to Heather, the gun pointed menacingly.

"You're just full of surprises," Heather said, raising her hands and stepping to the door.

Charlie pressed the gun into her back. "Don't even think about running. If they catch Zach and me, we'll face some time. But they're already about to lock you up and throw away the key—what do you think they'll do if they think you are trying to escape?" He raised his free arm and spoke into his wrist. "We're on the move, heading your way."

Zach followed Charlie and Heather out the door, trying to process what was happening. Charlie peeked around the hall corner but cursed under his breath. He quickly turned them around. "Maintenance guy is still working on the elevator. Back to the stairs."

"This is quite the escape plan you have here, Chaalee," Heather whispered.

As they approached the stairwell, voices could be heard up ahead. All three hurried through the stairwell door and moved against the wall. Charlie again leaned over the railing and listened. When it seemed clear, he motioned them to walk down.

"Are we going to crawl out a sewer pipe?" asked Heather. "Or do you have something even more spectacular planned?"

"Quiet," Charlie growled, as they descended toward the garage levels. As they passed the third floor, a door opened above them. Footsteps started clanging down. Charlie waved them down to the next level, but suddenly, Zach froze. Another electric pulse moved up his right side. His feet wouldn't budge and his legs collapsed. He grabbed at the metal railing to keep from tumbling down the stairwell.

When Charlie saw Zach crumpled on the stairs, he tugged Heather back to come help. She looked ready to struggle, but she relented and helped Charlie lift Zach's arms. Charlie nodded to a shadowy area under the stairwell with a maintenance door. "Quick, over there."

Zach slowly felt the sensation come back to his legs. He tried to support himself as Charlie and Heather pulled him into the darkness. The door was locked, so they pressed tightly against each other in the shadows. Zach could smell Heather's perfume. A strand of her hair draped over his ear. It was awkward being so close to a strange woman, especially when wearing only a hospital gown. He forced his mind back to the sound in the stairwell.

Zach didn't breathe as a man in a green military uniform stepped around the corner toward the next flight of stairs. The dark hiding space was out of view from the path of the stairs. As long as the man didn't turn and look directly at them, they should be fine. Zach could almost have reached out and touched the man as he passed the landing. But he didn't turn. He just opened the door and disappeared into the hallway.

"Chaalee," Heather whispered, "was that you getting fresh with me?"

Charlie ignored her and looked at Zach. "Are you okay? What happened?"

"Sorry," he answered. "I think I looked over the railing too quick. Just got dizzy."

Charlie motioned down the stairs. "Only a few more levels to the bottom. Can you walk?"

"Yeah," replied Zach. "Let's go."

"Just so I'm clear," said Heather, walking between them down the stairs, "what exactly is it you want with me?"

"I told you," Charlie whispered. "You're gonna help me get Bryce back across the bridge."

"And how am I going to do that?"

Charlie pushed open the door to the parking garage, looked both ways, and then stepped forward. "You know where Fitz is hiding and what they're planning. I'll bet you even know where they store the access codes for the execution sequences in the mainframe."

Heather stopped walking. "It's possible. What's in it for me?"

"You get to live," said Charlie, tightening his grip on the gun.

Heather laughed. "Please. You don't have it in you." She looked around the quiet garage, and then back at Charlie. "So, I get you what you need and you set me free?"

Zach wondered if this was Charlie's plan all along, or if grabbing Heather had been a spur of the moment addition. He couldn't believe that Tyler would take such a risk, but maybe he'd been the one to supply Charlie with the gun. Was there even room for all three of them to hide in the car?

Charlie nodded. "It's a deal."

Heather smiled. "I can point you to the central registry. From there you'll need to open the execution files that will reactivate the bridge."

"How do we do that?" asked Zach.

Heather smirked. "You don't. At least, not without the access codes. But as Chaalee guessed, I can get them for you."

A door banged from higher in the parking garage. "Come on." Charlie quickened his pace. "The car's right around the corner—"

He stopped on the other side of the concrete divider in the middle of the level. He stared back and forth and then raised his wrist. "Ty, come in." He shook his head. "I don't understand. He was right here."

Zach shivered in the colder garage. "Oh my gosh, it's freezing out here!"

Heather closed her eyes. "This is fabulous, Chaalee. You should have left me in my cell. I knew it was a mistake trusting my life to this clown show—"

It all happened in a flash.

Tires squealed. A dark car swerved around the concrete divider. A hand extended out the window. Was that a gun? A series of sharp pops sounded, and Charlie, Heather, and Zach dove for the ground.

Zach fell hard on the concrete floor. The car peeled away, its tires squealing up the ramp to the garage exit. Zach felt a pain at his hip. Had he been shot? He reached down and pulled his hand back. It was red with blood.

Charlie rose and stared at the blood on Zach's hand. "Are you all right? Were you hit?"

As Zach struggled to sit up, he realized the pain was just from where his hip had banged on the cement. But where was the blood coming from? He turned and saw Heather

Avanair lying still beside him. Her vacant eyes stared list-lessly at the ceiling. A dark red splotch spread across her left side. She was the one who'd been shot.

"Oh, no..." moaned Charlie as he felt for a pulse. He pulled his hand from her neck and stared back at Zach. "She's dead."

CHAPTER TWENTY_

T he sound of another engine pulled Zach out of his trance. Tyler's car swerved around the corner and skidded to a stop. He jumped out next to them and gawked at the scene. "What happened?"

"Someone pulled up and shot at us," cried Zach. He turned in a fury to Charlie, fists balled. "What are you trying to do? Get us all killed? Why did you stop for her in the first place? I thought you were trying to rescue me? Did you promise Bryce that you'd get her out too?"

Charlie shook his head silently, not seeming to know what to say.

Tyler put a hand on Zach's shoulder. "We have to go. If someone sees her, they'll lock this place down and we'll never get away." He stepped back to the open car door, but the other two stood frozen. "Guys, come on!"

Charlie finally turned and tapped Zach's arm. "Let's go. She's gone. There's nothing we can do."

Zach shook off Charlie's hand and pulled his gown over his knees. "Don't touch me." He climbed into the back seat of the car while Charlie sat up front with Tyler.

"They shouldn't check us going out like they did at the entrance, but lie down on the seat just in case, Zach, okay?" said Tyler. "I think there's a blanket you can cover yourself with too. Seeing someone in a hospital gown might draw some suspicion."

"You mean more suspicion than a dead body?" Zach stewed for a few seconds, but eventually he slid low in the seat. He found the blanket folded on the floorboards and wrapped it around his shoulders, immediately appreciating its warmth. No matter how mad he was at Charlie, he still didn't want to get stopped leaving the building. That wouldn't accomplish anything. He could scream later. Right now he just wanted to get out in one piece.

When they'd safely left the facility and turned onto the main road, Zach sat up in the back seat. Charlie tugged angrily on his tie. He lowered the window and threw it out. He looked over at Tyler. "What happened to you? Why did you move the car?"

"Security was circling the lower lot. I could tell he was eying me when he passed by the first time. I thought he was going to stop and question me on the second. When you still weren't out, I didn't want to be sitting there when he came by again."

"Sorry." Charlie rubbed his face with his hand. "I can't believe that just happened."

Zach kicked the back of the seat with his foot. "You can't believe it? You caused it to happen."

"Zach, try to take it easy," said Tyler. "Charlie may have gone off plan, but I don't think he meant to have her killed."

Charlie turned around to look at him. "I'm sorry. I heard General Weber talking to some people about you and Heather in the hallway when I was hiding in the supply closet outside your room. I'd seen her name listed on the intel Tyler pulled from Hendrickson. I'd copied down her room number just for kicks. When we left the stairwell and were suddenly on her floor, it just seemed right."

"It wasn't," huffed Zach. He saw the whole scene play out again in his mind. "If you hadn't planned to grab her, who was the other guy with the gun? Was he coming after her or us?"

Charlie shook his head. "No clue. It doesn't make sense. They couldn't have known we'd be there or that we'd have her. I guess they could have been trying to hit you, but maybe it was all just about Heather. I wouldn't put it past Yao to tie up loose ends, no matter how loyal those loose ends had been."

"Did she tell you anything?" asked Tyler. "Something we can use to help Bryce?"

Charlie shrugged. "Not much. She said the execution files for reactivating the bridge were in the central registry.

She was going to get us the access codes that would open the bridge, but now we'll have to find another way."

"Have you really been talking to Bryce?" asked Zach, staring at the scenery passing his window. Like everything else in his life, it was all just a blur. "Is he still okay?"

"I found where he's hiding in *Kingdom*," answered Charlie. "He breeched a secret underground computer lab. We think its access to Q2's mainframe will let us reactivate the bridge. You can talk to him if you want."

Zach whipped his head forward. "For real?"

Tyler nodded. "We're using a backchannel commlink. It's a little spotty, but he talked to Maggie for a few minutes last night."

Zach looked out the window again. "Where are we going? This isn't the road back to Milton."

"You can't go home," said Tyler. "They'll be looking for you there. For all of us."

"We're meeting up with Maggie, Andrew, and Jess," said Charlie. "I have a place we can hide while we finish the plan."

Zach leaned his head against the seat and closed his eyes. He wasn't sure these guys knew what they were doing, but he didn't have much choice but to follow along. It seemed like a lifetime ago that Bryce was at home. When their lives were normal. Now every minute that passed made it seem like Bryce was traveling farther and farther away from him. Zach had just about decided that the world would never be the same.

But if Bryce had a plan... maybe there was still a

chance. He'd always trusted that Bryce could do anything. Learning that he'd gotten mixed up in this disaster with Q2 had thrown Zach for a loop, but everyone made mistakes. If Bryce had a way to fix it, Zach was determined to trust him.

He had to.

CHAPTER TWENTY-ONE

Tyler pulled into a rest stop halfway up the mountain, parking next to Maggie's Explorer. "You made it!" Jess exclaimed as she ran over with Maggie and Andrew to greet them.

Maggie gave Zach a giant hug. "I'm so glad you're safe."

"Me too," he answered.

Andrew chuckled at Zach's shaved head and hospital gown. "Nice look you've got there, dude."

Zach worked to keep the gown over his legs as the wind blew at the edges. He felt his face turning red, even in the cold. He hated standing in the parking lot half-naked, especially in front of the girls.

"Here." Andrew reached back into the Explorer and pulled out a gym bag. "I brought a few extra clothes for myself, but you can wear them for now. Unless, you know, you want to stick with the 'hospital chic' vibe you're rocking. You could start a new trend. I'll bet all the kids at Milton would—"

Zach grabbed the bag and glared at him. "Shut up, will ya." He climbed in the back of the Explorer and quickly pulled on the new clothes. The sneakers were a little tight, but they were better than going barefoot, and it was good to finally wear something warm. He pulled out a flat-brimmed cap. "OLD FART," was plastered across the front. Zach shook his head and stepped back out to the parking lot.

"Sorry, that's all they had," Andrew said, grinning at the hat. "I bought it from inside the truck stop here after Tyler messaged us about your hair."

Zach couldn't help cracking up too. "It's fine. Anything's better than that gown."

Maggie suggested they stop at the Wal-Mart up the road for supplies. They needed some food and equipment if they were to be hiding out for a few days. Zach hadn't heard the full plan, but some food sounded good for sure.

Tyler charged everything on his credit card, and they wheeled two large shopping carts into the parking lot. They'd purchased gallon jugs of water, bread, peanut butter and jelly, various other food items that didn't need to be refrigerated or cooked, flashlights, sleeping bags, and a portable heater since Charlie said it was cold up on the mountain at night.

Zach picked out a few extra clothes and some cheap sneakers that fit better. Andrew pointed to a wider variety of hats, but he decided to keep the goofy one. After everything that had happened, it felt good to laugh.

After much discussion, they agreed to ditch Tyler's car in the Wal-Mart parking lot since it was likely on camera after breaking into the government building. Maggie handed Charlie the keys to her Explorer. "I've had enough harrowing trips along those mountain roads for one lifetime. Besides, you're the only one who knows exactly where we're heading."

She squeezed into the backseat, shoulder to shoulder with Jess, Andrew, and Zach. Tyler sat in the front next to Charlie. There really wasn't enough room, but it was easier to only have one vehicle. They couldn't risk being nabbed by the cops.

While Charlie drove up the mountain, Tyler explained to the others what had happened. "Oh my god," Maggie whispered when she heard how Heather had been gunned down. "I didn't mean it when I said I wanted her dead. That's terrible."

"But none of you were hurt?" asked Jess.

Zach shook his head. "Not yet."

"So how exactly is this going to work?" asked Andrew. "You really think you can sneak us into Q2's building? Isn't it on lockdown? You know, sealed up tight with that yellow tape or something. It's probably crawling with Weber's people."

"They're guarding the entrance," said Charlie, "but like I told you before, I found a back way in. No one actually goes inside. Besides, it's an abandoned section of the complex where I've been hiding out."

"It's our best option," said Tyler. "We can't go home. They'll be looking for us all now."

"We're fugitives," moaned Andrew. "I can't believe it."

"Hiding right under their noses might just be so obvious that they won't think to look," said Jess. "It's pretty smart, actually."

Charlie grinned. "Thanks."

Zach shook his head. "Let's not get ahead of ourselves."

They all sent messages to their parents, explaining that they were safe but had to go away for a few days. It was certain to freak them all out, but it was unavoidable. They explained that they had something very important to do, and that they loved them.

Tyler had them immediately power down their phones so they wouldn't be tracked. "Don't use them again unless it's an emergency," he warned.

"At least this way we won't see their reactions," said Maggie as she put her phone away.

"My mom will never understand," said Andrew, shaking his head.

"None of them will," said Jess. "But hopefully someday they'll understand that we were working for something really important."

"Like getting Bryce back," said Zach.

"We have to stop these people," added Charlie.

"There's more going on than any of us understand. All our futures could be at risk," said Tyler as they wound up the mountain. "Remember the cosmic abnormalities I told you about at lunch in the café?"

"Yeah," said Andrew.

"Well…" said Tyler. "They've been growing."

"That sounds bad," said Jess.

Tyler nodded. "It's certainly not good. The scientists don't know why it's happening or what will happen if it continues."

"We have to get Bryce home," said Maggie.

Charlie tapped his hand on the dashboard. "And then we'll shut it down. All of it. Once and for all."

Everyone seemed to let the news sink in as darkness fell. The curvy mountain roads brought back so many memories to Zach. He could almost see the Ranger perched on the roof of Maggie's Jeep, ripping through the canvas top and dragging him from his seat. As he remembered the attack, an electric pulse suddenly shot through his body. His shoulder burned at the spot where the Ranger's tight grip had dug into his skin.

Maggie seemed to notice his body tensing. "Are you okay?"

Zach nodded, gritting his teeth until the sensation passed. "Yeah, just a cramp," he lied. The episodes were getting worse, both in frequency and intensity. The incident in the stairwell had only been a few hours ago. Now he'd had another one in the car. They'd never happened that close together before. He didn't want anyone else to worry. Bryce's situation was much more important than his. Zach thought he'd deflected Charlie's concern by saying he'd been dizzy on the stairs, but it would be hard to hide this from everyone if they kept happening so often. They seemed to happen in stressful situations, but stress was one thing he couldn't seem to avoid these days.

Charlie slowed and then turned onto a narrow dirt trail. "Hold on, this is gonna get bumpy." He continued a little farther and then plowed the Explorer straight into the woods. Branches and small twigs scraped at the windshield and sides of the vehicle.

"Geez, dude," exclaimed Andrew, pushing hard against the others in the backseat as he leaned away from the window.

"There goes the paint job," muttered Maggie.

"Sorry about that," said Charlie. "But the car needs to stay out of sight. We don't want anyone stumbling onto it." He shut off the engine and opened the door. "There shouldn't be anyone out here at night, but let's stay quiet just in case." They emptied from the car, and everyone from the backseat stretched after the tight squeeze.

Charlie turned on a flashlight but kept it trained close to the ground by his feet. "Watch your step and stay in a single-file line behind me. It's a few minutes to the building entrance, but I've memorized the way."

It was creepy walking through the darkness. The moon gave just enough illumination so they could see Charlie's outline behind his flashlight beam. They skulked through the trees like a silent line of ants or a secret invasion party. Zach knew they were somewhere on the back side of the mountain, but he'd never been to the Q2 compound. There were so many questions he wanted answered. His pulse quickened as he thought about communicating again with Bryce.

Charlie held up a hand and stopped before a tall, chain-link fence. Zach saw the dark shadow of a building on the other side. Charlie reached down and carefully disconnected a tripwire he'd set outside a break in the fence. He said it was an early warning system he'd rigged to alert him if anyone was coming. It ran through a broken window in the building and was attached to a metal bell he'd set up inside.

He lifted the broken fence section and ducked under-neath. Then he held the opening as everyone crawled through one at a time. When they were all inside the fence, Charlie reattached the tripwire before guiding them to a smaller, one-story, brick section at the back of the hulking complex.

At the base of the wall, Charlie knelt and brushed away a patch of leaves from a wooden board that he lifted and set gently against the brick wall. He shone his light into what seemed to be the opening of a ground-level window with all its glass busted out before whispering something to Tyler and then lowering his feet through the hole and disap-pearing out of sight.

A moment later, he shined his light back through the opening. He motioned for the rest of them to follow, and one by one, everyone slipped through the window. Zach landed inside after Maggie and then helped Tyler down as he replaced the wooden covering.

Charlie raised his light, shining it around what looked like an old storeroom that hadn't been touched in decades.

"Keep your voices down, but I think we're okay. It doesn't look like anyone else has been in here since I left, and the patrols never check my hideout."

"You've been living here?" asked Andrew.

"Not right here. Follow me, I'll show you." Charlie led them through a connecting hallway to another room further inside the building. "Hang on, I'll get the lights," he said as he cracked open a metal box on the far wall. There was a clicking sound before two lights slowly grew brighter in the ceiling. He must have flipped on a breaker switch.

"Voila," he proclaimed.

The room was roughly the size of one of Zach's classrooms back in Milton. Several tables and stacks of chairs were pushed against one wall, while rows of shelves with file boxes and odd assortments of junk lined another. "What is this place?" he asked.

"It used to be an old Tech building, I think," answered Charlie. "I found a bunch of envelopes and papers with 'School of Agriculture' printed on them, but that must have been ages ago." He pointed toward the other end of the hallway from where they'd entered. "The main Q2 complex is down there a ways, past some fire doors to the other building. No one seems to come over here. You can't see these lights from the outside, I checked. So, as long as we stay quiet, we should be safe."

Zach walked to a collection of new electronic equipment set up on the table. He glanced back at Charlie. "These computers were here too?"

Charlie grinned. "No, I brought those in. I made some

scavenging trips out to the Q2 lab. Nothing like building a DIY programming space. It's amazing how much you can do with a hand-truck, a power source, and some high-speed cables."

Andrew lifted a metal chair from a stack against the wall. He blew off a thick layer of dust and coughed before sitting down. "It's kind of a dump."

"It'll work great," said Maggie, shaking her head at Andrew. "Nice job, Charlie."

"Thanks."

Tyler examined the table with the computers, tracing the cables to where they disappeared into the wall. He turned to Charlie. "We might need to set up a few more workstations, maybe put a monitor along the wall, but this could work."

Zach studied the electronics and then looked back at Tyler and Charlie. "You said I could talk to Bryce. Can we do that now?"

Charlie nodded. "Give me a little time to get tapped in to the mainframe again." He put his hand on Zach's shoulder. "We'll get him back."

CHAPTER TWENTY-TWO

B ryce exhaled at the top of a push-up along the floor of the lab. With his leg wound healing nicely, he'd made a habit of stopping his coding work every few hours to exercise. There were limits to how long he could sit at a computer, and moving around helped his mind stay sharp. He wished he could swim in the pool on the other side of the waterfall, but he had no desire to face the creature again. Instead, he ran laps around the outer aisles of the lab and did sit-ups, push-ups, and stretches. He imagined he was late for practice and Coach Simmons was riding him hard. It wasn't the same, but it was another trick to point his mind toward normalcy.

When Bryce was living at the oasis, he'd had a routine for recording the days. He'd logged each new dawn with a mark on a rock beside the peaceful stream that trickled down the canyon walls. He'd reached forty-seven marks before Zach came across the bridge. Of course, there had been more before he'd reached the desert, and more before Rachel had been gunned down by the Rangers, but it was something. He knew time didn't progress the same in *Kingdom* as it did back home, but knowing how long he had been gone, in any way, gave him a sense of normalcy.

Since Zach had gone back through the portal, Bryce hadn't had the luxury of living in the same place long enough to establish a routine. Life on the run was one frantic step after the next. The Rangers had been hunting him like prey. Now, deep underground, he no longer saw the sky. The suns never rose and set. He spent nearly every waking hour the same way—poring over lines of code. So he'd never picked up the practice of tracking the time down in the lab. Instead, he spent all his time carefully constructing the sequences that would power the plan he'd concocted with Charlie.

Fitz had done a lot of the legwork. It had taken Bryce a few hours of staring at the hologram, watching Fitz build the long scroll of his sequences, but eventually Bryce had figured it out. Fitz was building another bridge. Well, not another one, exactly. He was modifying the code from Eden, turning it on its head to allow access to the real-world side of the bridge without the need for enormous machines like Eden and JOSHUA. In theory, his code would create the ability to open the bridge at specific locations back on Earth; portal points just like the cave pool, the grain silo, the chasm, and the Central Plateau on the *Kingdom* side. So if Bryce could hijack Fitz's code, it might allow him to open the bridge long enough to get himself back home.

The ability to port into the virtual world from multiple places back on earth would be a game changer. Yao and his minions could create as many entry points as they wanted into *Kingdom*, or maybe even other dimensions beyond this virtual world, without the expense of building a machine. Charlie had quickly agreed that such technology was far too dangerous for Yao, or anyone else, to possess. Once Bryce crossed, they had to destroy it.

He wondered if his image showed through to Fitz, just as Charlie's had when Bryce had seen him for the first time at the other workstation. There was no way to know, but it seemed like Fitz would have reacted or sounded the alarm if he had noticed Bryce was there. Maybe he already had. Rangers could be on their way to stop him. But it didn't matter. He had to keep going.

Bryce wasn't just racing against Fitz. The glitches he'd experienced inside *Kingdom* with the boulder on the river and the unusual patches in the night sky were troubling. Something was changing in the world, and there was no telling how it might affect the bridge or his ability to get home.

As he finished his workout, he stretched out flat along the floor. A row of cardboard tubes that he hadn't noticed before were stacked against the wall. He wiped the sweat from his forehead and opened one. Rolls of paper poured out, and as Bryce flattened them, he saw they were building schematics, like blueprints. He opened several tubes until he found drawings he recognized as the plans for his underground lab. He spread them across the cement, studying the extensive network of tunnels and passageways. Now that he could see the route he'd taken from the outer cave all mapped out, it was a miracle he'd ever found the place. He noticed a vertical corridor, like an escape tunnel, on the opposite side of the lab from where he'd entered from the pool.

He moved a cabinet to gain clear access to the wall that was next to the corridor on the schematic. He searched for an opening, or a ladder perhaps, but the wall seemed solid. Then he saw the rectangular shape of an access panel. The metal cover slid open at his touch, revealing a round button. It could do anything, Bryce realized, but his curiosity overwhelmed his caution, and he pushed it. A portion of the wall magically shifted to the left, revealing a small, closet-sized room. He stepped inside. It was an elevator.

If the schematic plans were correct, the passage ran straight up to the surface. Bryce had a sudden longing to see the sky and breathe fresh air. He pushed the lone button on the interior panel and the door slid shut. Soon he was moving steadily upward through the layers of rock.

Bryce expected to have to shield his eyes from the bright sunlight, but when the door finally opened, he stood frozen. Something was very wrong. This wasn't the landscape that he'd left when he'd entered the cave. He could tell from the dual suns high in the sky that it was daytime, but the light barely shone through a thick haze. A foul taste, like sulfur, hit his mouth from the breeze.

He was so caught up staring at the scene, he almost

didn't notice the elevator door closing. He blocked it with his arm at the last moment and then looked for a way to prop it open. The control panel in the elevator only had the single button, which he presumed would take him back to the lab. If he walked outside, he might not be able to get the door back open once it shut.

Bryce placed a foot in the door track and leaned out. He spied a large branch that he thought he could reach. He dragged the branch to the doorway, propping it on the track. The door tried to close again, but bounced back open when it hit the wood. The branch was sturdy enough that it should give him enough time to inspect the surface.

Bryce stepped out of the elevator and turned around. The doorway was built into the side of a mountain, partially hidden by branches and leaves. He'd likely walk straight past it if he didn't know it was there. He couldn't find an access panel in the rock and was immediately glad he'd propped the door open.

Across from the mountain was a wide field scattered with trees. He could just make out water in the distance, probably the river he'd traveled in.

The sky looked angry, like the cloud formations he'd seen created twice before when the bridge had opened, once at the chasm and once at the desert pool. Thunder echoed in the distance, and the wind was quickly growing in strength. The air felt thin, like the oxygen was slowly being squeezed from the atmosphere. Sulfur still burned in his mouth, and it felt like it was penetrating down into his lungs. Was this all a result of the bridge opening and closing, or had it been caused by the modifications he and Fitz were making to the code on the mainframe?

Discovering the underground lab may have saved him in more ways than he'd imagined. He may not have made it much longer if he'd had to breathe such toxic air up on the surface. He coughed, his lungs burning, and stepped back into the elevator.

He had to get back. Time was running out.

CHAPTER TWENTY-THREE_

A n alert was blinking on his computer terminal when Bryce got back to the lab. It was a transmission request from Charlie on the network comm. Bryce hoped they'd been successful in rescuing Zach and were now safely in hiding. He'd have to update them on what he'd seen on the surface. They weren't just racing to beat Fitz and the others at Q2; they were now battling the virtual world of *Kingdom* itself. He'd always planned to leave—now he had to.

Bryce selected the neighboring terminal to his workstation to transmit the hologram. Charlie had hacked a circuitous route along the back channels of the mainframe to connect them. They were betting that Q2 wouldn't notice it so far off the beaten path. It was crazy, but somehow it worked. When the connection was secure, a faint light slowly flickered into the shape of a figure at the next desk. Bryce smiled in surprise when the hologram appeared. It was Zach.

"Hey, brother," Bryce called. "It's so good to see you."

"Oh my gosh, Bryce!" Zach answered. "How are you?"

"Surviving."

Zach laughed nervously.

"Sorry I bailed on you back at the chasm," Bryce said.

"Bailed? It wasn't your fault. The Sportsman had you." Zach's voice caught, and he wiped a tear. "I didn't think I'd ever see you again."

Bryce grinned. "Come on, you know it takes more than a fly rod to keep me down." He stared at Zach's appearance through the hologram. He was wearing a flat-brimmed trucker's hat, with words across the front. The image was slightly blurred, but he thought it read OLD FART. He laughed. "Nice hat!"

"Yeah," said Zach, chuckling as he lifted the hat. "That's nothing, check this out." His hair was shaved nearly to the scalp.

"What happened?" asked Bryce. "You get in a fight with a weed-whacker?"

"Don't ask. But I'm never going back to that hospital." Zach looked off to the side. "Here, someone else wants to say hi." He stepped away, and Maggie appeared in the stream.

For a moment Bryce just stared at her beautiful face, remembering the feel of her hair that hung over her shoulder, a strand catching the top of her ear. He closed his eyes.

It seemed like a lifetime ago that they'd sat together up on the water tower and he'd given her the necklace.

"Bryce, are you there?"

He looked up and smiled. "Hey, babe."

"I miss you so much," she replied.

He nodded. "Is Charlie with you? Are you all back at the compound?"

Maggie nodded and scooted just out of view to make room for Charlie. "I'm here, Bryce. Yes, we made it back." He brought Bryce up to speed with their coding progress, how they'd broken Zach out of the facility, and Heather's death.

Bryce's eyes opened wide. "Shot? By who?"

"I don't know," Charlie answered. "It all happened so fast. We couldn't tell if he was aiming for her or for us. But she's gone."

Bryce tried to process the news. "I didn't know you were planning to grab Heather."

"We weren't," said Tyler, leaning into view.

"It was a spur-of-the-moment decision," explained Charlie. "I thought she might have information that could help us open the bridge."

"Did she?"

Charlie hesitated. "Sort of." He shared what she'd told them about the execution files in the central registry. "But that was all we got."

Bryce frowned. "That's not much."

"I know, sorry," Charlie answered. "She said she could get us the codes too, but she never had the chance."

Zach leaned into the transmission. "Does it help? I mean, can we use that information in any way to get closer to activating the bridge?"

"Maybe," said Bryce, thinking it through as they spoke. He'd nearly finished building upon the sequences he'd stolen from Fitz. The execution files were the final step. "At least now I know where to look. I'll just have to crack them, but it would have been easier to get the access codes."

As Bryce was talking, he noticed Zach's face take on a pained expression. Suddenly, Zach grabbed his head and rocked forward. "Zach?" Bryce cried.

He saw Maggie and Charlie in the edges of the hologram pulling Zach by the shoulders, but it was hard to tell exactly what was happening. Their rapid motion skipped through the holographic stream like a scratched DVD.

"What's happening?" Bryce called. "What's wrong with him?"

Maggie slid into the stream. "It's okay. He's lying down now. Jess and Andrew are with him. He was feeling dizzy."

"Has this happened before?" asked Bryce, gripping the edge of the table.

Maggie shared how Zach had acted in the car. "But he said it was a leg cramp, so I didn't think much of it."

Charlie's face leaned in close to Maggie's. "He had an episode in the stairwell too when we were breaking him out."

Maggie turned in surprise. "He did?"

Charlie nodded. "He said he was dizzy from looking

over the stairwell. I believed him, but I guess I should have said something."

Bryce shook his head. "Why's he hiding it? What's happening to him?"

Maggie moved to the side, and Tyler came into frame. "Bryce, it's possible that it has something to do with crossing the bridge, or at least with the disturbances we have been reading since the bridges were activated. The discoloration in his hair also seems to be spreading. Have you had any similar symptoms?"

Bryce shook his head. As much as everything felt weird and abnormal inside *Kingdom*, he hadn't had any pains or dizzy spells, and as far as he could tell, his hair was normal. He told them what he'd seen up on the surface. "The atmosphere is crumbling. We don't have much time."

He closed his eyes. He'd been ready to sacrifice himself at the chasm portal to get Zach back across. Now, even though Zach was home, he might still be sick. All because of him. It was bad enough that he was trapped inside this nightmare, but what haunted Bryce the most was that he'd also endangered everyone he cared about. He'd thought Charlie was gone, but amazingly he'd survived. He'd already lost Rachel. If something happened to Zach, Bryce would never forgive himself.

While the others attended to Zach, Bryce reviewed the programming sequences with Charlie and Tyler. "We need to select the two end points. They'll be the access portals that will send me out of here and back to you."

"Like the pool in the cave where Zach landed?" asked Tyler.

"Exactly," said Bryce. "But that's a long way from here. With the air like it is on the surface, I don't think I'd make it. There's a pool here next to the lab…" He glanced over his shoulder. The electric pool beyond the waterfall was larger than the pool in the canyon cave, but there was no opening in the ceiling, just layer after layer of rock. And his mind went back to the creature. "It's just that—"

"What?" asked Tyler.

Bryce's eyes fell to the lab schematics still spread across the floor. He reached for them and then traced the drawing of the elevator shaft with his finger as it rose to the surface. It just might work.

He looked back at the hologram. "I might have something. There's an elevator shaft. But we need to come up with a place on your end. Can you get the Eden machine working in the compound?"

Charlie shook his head. "It's a no-go. Eden's toast. Q2 sabotaged a lot of their own equipment on their way out and the military took anything it thought worth examining. It would take weeks to get something running again, and we don't have that kind of time."

"Then you'll need to pull its coordinate sensors," said Bryce. "I found some here in the lab that should work on my end. Can you get to the Eden machine and scavenge the sensors?"

"We can try," said Tyler. "The military has guards posted

24/7 outside the main entrance to the compound, but we can sneak through the building to get to the main lab."

Bryce nodded, ticking off the list of outstanding items in his head. "Now you just need a place to put them. A space that's conducive to receiving the transport."

"What did you and Rachel pass into when you entered *Kingdom*?" asked Charlie. "Was it the same cave pool as Zach?"

"It was at the country farm," said Bryce. "We came through into a grain silo. The Rangers torched the silo when Rachel and I were fleeing. But something like that could work for you."

Maggie leaned into the stream, her fingers holding something toward him. The necklace. "Bryce, what about the water tower? It's like a grain silo and a pool rolled into one."

It just might work. "But it's back in Milton," said Bryce. "Aren't you all up in the mountains at the Q2 compound?"

"That's even better," said Maggie. "We'd be back home when you got here and not right next to a military guard."

Charlie leaned back into the stream. "The tower's also a perfect, secluded place to hide out until the bridge opens. I noticed a utility substation just through the woods when I spent time here before. We should be able to use that for a power source. We'll just need to get the sensors and finish the programming from here first."

"Bryce," said Tyler, "do you think you'll be able to start the activation sequence from your side?"

"Yeah, if I can break the codes, it should actually work better that way."

"Then it's settled," said Charlie. "Now it just has to work. Other than that, it's easy-peasy."

"Right." Bryce chuckled, remembering how much he'd enjoyed Charlie's sense of humor before Yao's goons had drugged him.

Zach's face appeared back on the edge of the transmission. He looked tired, and Tyler moved so Zach could sit in the chair.

"You okay, buddy?" asked Bryce.

Zach nodded. "I don't know what's happening. I thought these spells would go away, but they're getting worse. I should have said something."

Bryce wiped his face with his hands. "Zach, it's just that—"

Zach held up his index finger. "Listen, don't worry about me. You guys have to keep going and fix this. Please."

Charlie nodded. "He's right, Bryce. It might be the only way to help him. To help everyone."

CHAPTER TWENTY-FOUR_

After the communication with Bryce, Tyler divided the group into three project teams, each with specific tasks to complete. Tyler would stay at the computers, working to synch Bryce's work on the programming sequences with the computers in the real world so that both sides would be ready for the bridge activation. Andrew and Jess agreed to sneak back to the Explorer to retrieve the remaining jugs of drinking water and any other bits that had been left in the car. Charlie helped them climb out the window, and he disconnected the end of the tripwire from the warning bell until they made it back. Zach and Maggie would go with Charlie deeper into the compound to scavenge the coordinate sensors from the Eden machine.

Maggie put her hand on Zach's shoulder while they waited for Charlie to return from letting Jess and Andrew out of the building. "Maybe you should stay here and rest."

He pushed her hand away. "What are you talking about? I'm fine."

"You're not fine."

Zach frowned. "Well, I'm still coming with you. I don't need to be treated like a baby."

"I'm just worried about you, that's all," said Maggie. "We don't know what's causing those spells."

Zach sighed. He didn't know precisely what was causing them either, but it didn't matter. He had to help with the final preparations to activate the portal. Lying on the floor wouldn't accomplish that. "I'm coming," he said defiantly.

"It's this way." Charlie pointed down the dark hallway to their left. Maggie grabbed Zach's hand before giving him a look that said he'd better not argue.

"I found a fire door that was unlocked," said Charlie. "We can use that to get into the main corridor to the lab. I haven't seen guards on the inside this time of day, but let's stay silent just in case."

As Charlie had described, their hideout room was in an auxiliary building, long- abandoned from the early days of Tech. Now, the whole place looked like something out of a horror movie. Most of the emergency lights along the ceiling were out. The few that still functioned flickered on and off, casting eerie shadows over the abandoned halls. It was as if everyone that was supposed to be there had just vanished.

They soon came to the fire door. Charlie opened it just enough for them to slip through, but a deep creaking sound echoed along the cement block walls. After a series of turns, they stopped outside the main lab. A noise clanged somewhere from deep within the building. They all froze, listening for approaching footsteps, but no one came.

Charlie led them into the lab, stopping at a landing with a metal railing. It looked out across an open room the size of a small gymnasium. The ceiling was high, and a series of tables and desks lined the room in rows. Near the far wall stood a robust metal object, like a cement mixer but more space-aged. Even in the dim light, its silver surface looked like it was about to blast off to some distant planet.

Not too far from the truth, Zach thought, immediately recognizing its similarity to the device he'd entered back in Hendrickson's cavern. It was the Eden machine. A shiver ran down his spine as he remembered the unbearable forces that had shuttled his molecules across the dimensions. He felt short of breath but casually grabbed the railing so Charlie and Maggie wouldn't notice.

"Come on," Charlie whispered. "Stay close."

They walked up the aisle between the rows of computer workstations. Charlie pointed out Fitz's desk and the mainframe that had once controlled the central systems. The Eden machine loomed before them like a sleeping iron giant.

"This is where it all happened," whispered Charlie. He stepped into a spot on the polished cement floor between the mainframe and the Eden machine. "I thought I would make it. Bryce and Rachel were already in the chamber…" He glanced at the entrance door, a faraway look in his eyes. "Even when Fitz and the others stormed the lab, only a few seconds were left on the countdown sequence. They were too late. I was going to make it in."

Zach and Maggie listened silently as he played the scene back. "I didn't count on the gun." Charlie shook his head and stepped to his left. "This is where they shot me. There was nothing I could do. I just lay here on the floor and watched the chamber door close. The last thing I heard was Fitz's cursing as Bryce and Rachel vanished. Then I blacked out."

Maggie reached over and touched Charlie's shoulder. "It's okay. You did everything you could."

He shook his head. "That's the thing... I didn't. You don't know." He looked up at them with tears in his eyes. "I betrayed them."

"What do you mean?" asked Zach.

"Before that, I gave up. I turned them over to Yao. I thought he'd just let us go. You know, send us home for refusing to take part in his plans." He glanced up at the Eden machine. "I never thought all this could happen."

The anger was mounting again inside Zach's heart. What was he saying? That Bryce could have been saved if not for Charlie's betrayal? He felt his emotions rising like they had back at the hospital when Charlie had stopped at Heather Avanair's room. What was wrong with him?

He was about to lash out, but Maggie reached out again and squeezed his hand. "No one could have predicted that all this would happen," she said softly to Charlie. "You did the best you could. And you're making up for it now."

Charlie wiped his cheeks. "Bryce has been in there all this time. And Rachel... It's all my fault."

Maggie nodded for Zach to say something. He took a deep breath, trying to push back his fury. She was right. It wasn't any more Charlie's fault than it was Bryce's. All that mattered now was fixing things. "It's okay. Come on, we've got a job to do. Show us where the coordinate sensors are, we need to get—"

A sound echoed from the hallway outside the lab entrance. There was no mistaking the noise now. Someone was definitely coming.

"Quick!" hissed Charlie. "Hide!" All three ran behind the Eden machine, ducking out of sight just as the lab doors opened. A military guard entered from the hallway, a machine gun in his hands. Zach had an eerie recollection of the Rangers chasing him and Bryce toward the chasm.

They didn't move as the soldier patrolled the aisles. He hadn't seen them. He was just making his rounds, doing a routine security check of the building. They'd just need to stay hidden until he left, so long as he didn't wander to their side of the machine.

Zach's heart was racing again. He leaned against the smooth, silvery Eden machine to rest. But when his skin touched the metal, a jolt of electricity shot through him. It darted from the right side of his skull all the way to his toes. A flash of green filled his vision, and he suddenly saw himself sailing through space across the bridge. The image disappeared as quickly as it had come. He tried to pull back, but he felt paralyzed. Tiny tremors pulsated through his stiffened limbs. Zach opened his mouth to tell Maggie and Charlie what has happening, but he couldn't make a sound. His mouth was bone dry.

Finally, Maggie turned and noticed his pained expression. She nudged Charlie, and they quickly reached out to grab Zach's shoulders, moving him away from contact with the Eden machine. A faint moan fell from Zach's lips as he lay flat on the cement floor, but Maggie quickly covered his mouth with her hand. His body felt numb, but he had a clear view of the lab from a gap underneath the machine. The guard had stopped halfway down an aisle. Had he heard them? The man peered around the room, testing the silence for signs of trouble.

Drool slipped from Zach's mouth onto Maggie's hand and the floor. He thought he might vomit, but he held it back with whatever control he still had of his body. The pain was far worse than it had been during any other episode. Had he flashed back to his trip across the bridge? What was happening to him? After all he'd been through, was this how he would die?

The guard pivoted back toward the entrance, finishing his sweep of the outer aisles. He paused for one last glance around the room and then walked back out to the hallway. The door closed with a thud.

Maggie removed her hand from Zach's mouth and stared into his eyes. Her face was panicked.

"Zach, can you hear me?" she cried. "Is he breathing?"

Charlie lowered his ear to Zach's chest. "I think so."

"Don't do this to us, Zach," Maggie cried. "I'm not losing you too."

Zach slowly felt the pain subside. He blinked, then he moved his fingers and discovered he could nod his head. He struggled to find his voice. "I'm okay," he eked out.

Maggie covered her face. "Oh, thank god."

The feeling crept back into his body like a wave of warmth flowing from his toes up to his head. With Charlie's help, he sat up and leaned against Maggie's shoulder.

Zach turned to the machine. "The pain hit me when I touched the metal." He slid over to lean against the wall. "I'll rest over here."

"Are you sure?" asked Maggie.

"Yeah." Zach nodded, his breathing gradually returning to normal. "I'm all right now. You guys keep going. We have to finish."

Maggie kept glancing back at him to make sure he didn't fall into another episode as Charlie directed her to the front control panel. They located the coordinate sensors, and with a little effort and a few tools from a maintenance bench, they extracted several round discs and cables. Charlie didn't look happy as they dragged the thick black cables over to the wall.

"What's wrong?" Zach asked.

"I think one of the sensor discs broke when I pried it loose," Charlie answered. "The screwdriver went right through the center."

"Will it still work?" asked Maggie.

Charlie bit his lip. "I can't tell. Tyler will need to look at them."

Maggie looked back at Zach. "Can you walk?"

Zach nodded as he pulled himself to his feet. "I think so."

"What'll we do if they don't work?" asked Maggie.

Charlie shook his head. "I guess we'll move to Plan B."

"What's Plan B?" asked Zach.

"We don't have one," Charlie answered grimly.

CHAPTER TWENTY-FIVE

When they returned to the hideout, Jess and Andrew were huddled around the computer with Tyler. Two water jugs sat on the floor next to the remaining food supplies.

"No problems at the car?" asked Charlie.

Jess nodded at Andrew. "Only him."

"Hey," said Andrew, looking insulted. "Next time you can carry them by yourself."

"I *did*..." Jess huffed, rolling her eyes.

"That was only for a second." Andrew touched his ribs. "I told you, I got a cramp."

"I've got one too," said Jess. "It's you."

"You didn't see anyone in the woods?" asked Charlie, stopping at the doorway on his way to reattach the tripwire. "No sign of anyone looking for us?"

"Nah," said Andrew. "And the Explorer's shoved into those bushes tight. You'd bang into it before you saw it."

"I think we're safe," agreed Jess. "How'd it go for you guys?" She glanced at Zach, who had slumped in a chair. "Is he okay? Did something happen?"

"He had another spell," answered Maggie.

"Worse than the others," said Charlie.

Zach shook his head. "I'm right here, you know. You don't have to talk like I'm not in the room. I'm not dead yet."

"Zach, don't say that," Maggie cried.

"That's not funny, dude," Andrew added. "We're just worried about you, that's all."

Zach pointed to Charlie's backpack. "Why don't you worry about the sensors. They're the only things that will end all this."

Tyler turned from his work. "Did you find what we needed?"

"Yeah." Charlie reached for the mass of cables on the floor. "But I damaged one of the sensors with my damn screwdriver." He lifted the third sensor from the pack, grimacing as he stuck a finger through the middle.

"That's not good," said Tyler.

"Sorry," said Charlie. "They were wedged in there tight."

"How do we use these, anyway?" Andrew picked up one of the undamaged discs. "They look like the woofers from my dad's old stereo speakers. He gave them to me before he moved to San Antonio."

"We use them very carefully," answered Tyler, taking the sensor from Andrew's grasp. "Each disc helps triangulate the coordinates for the portal beam. They get placed like this."

He positioned each one on the floor to create a triangle pattern. "The three sensors connect through the cables to create a target. It's like an electrical net to catch the transmission from the bridge. They're normally hidden inside the larger construct of the Eden machine. JOSHUA has a set just like them. But the program Bryce has modified from Fitz will allow us to direct the bridge to the sensors independent of a machine. We'll position this net on the water tower, which will serve as our apparatus to receive the beam."

"Like the pool in the cave," said Zach, watching the demonstration from his chair.

"Exactly," said Tyler. "Or the grain silo or the chasm."

"But what if the sensor's really broken?" asked Jess. "Will it work with only two?"

Tyler frowned. "That's the thing. To create an opening, we need at least three coordinate points. Otherwise it's just a flat line. I'm not sure what would happen if we tried to receive a transmission like that. It might…"

"What?" asked Maggie.

"I don't know," Tyler admitted. "But it could be like running into a brick wall for whatever is coming through." They all stared at the discs on the ground and considered what that would mean. "But I'll see if I can fix it," Tyler said, optimistically. "I have a few ideas that might work."

For the next few hours, Charlie worked on finalizing the coding, while Tyler tried to repair the coordinate sensor. Jess spotted an old soldering kit on the shelves that Tyler thought might help. She also found an old box-shaped television set on a rolling cart that was in the next room, with a dusty set of rabbit-ear antennas attached to the top. Jess wheeled it over and plugged it in. She twisted the antenna in different directions until a picture came into view. Zach recognized the man and woman sitting at the desk on the screen. They were the anchors at Channel 6. It was the Milton evening news.

His family never used to watch the news until Bryce disappeared. Since then it had become a regular staple in his house, one of his parents' ways of keeping informed about any clues about their son. Static filtered in and out of the picture, but then the view changed to the familiar scene of Zach's front yard.

"Dude, it's your house," shouted Andrew. "Turn it up!"

Jess adjusted the volume knob, and as a reporter spoke, the camera switched to show Zach's living room. His mom and dad were sitting together on the couch. Zach caught his breath at a close-up on his parents' faces. It was almost too much to watch, but he couldn't turn away.

"I'm sitting here with Kevin and Stacy Pearson, the parents of Bryce Pearson, the Milton High School student who went missing last fall. In a tragic turn of events, the Pearsons' younger son, thirteen-year-old Zach, has now gone missing as well."

The reporter swiveled and stuck the microphone under his mom's nose. "Mrs. Pearson, what does a mother feel when both of her boys go missing?"

Maggie moved next to Zach and squeezed his hand gently.

"Zach didn't disappear," his mom answered, indignantly. "He was taken from us three nights ago. Straight from this couch. Government agents stormed in and took him away. There was nothing we could do."

The reporter looked shocked. "Just to clarify, Mrs. Pearson, you believe that the government has taken your youngest son?"

His mom nodded. "That's right."

"What about your son Bryce? Mr. Pearson, do you believe the government took him as well?"

Zach's dad shook his head. "We don't know. But Zach seemed to have information. He was about to tell us something important, when they took him."

The reporter glanced back at the camera. "And if that's not enough, the Pearsons tell me that in addition to their two boys, the whereabouts of four other area youths are also in question. Two of Zach's classmates at Milton Middle School, Andrew Gordon and Jessica Barnes, as well as Jessica's brother, twenty-three-year-old Tyler Barnes, a graduate assistant at Tech, and Milton High School senior and Bryce Pearson's girlfriend, Maggie Palmer, are all currently missing."

The reporter turned back to the couch. "Mr. and Mrs. Pearson, all these young people know each other. Is there a connection between their disappearances?"

"There's no doubt in our mind," Zach's dad answered.

"We don't know how or why," added his mom, staring directly into the camera. "We just want our boys home. All the children. We just want them all to come home. Please, if you have them, or you have any information about their whereabouts, please tell us."

The camera panned out from the couch as the reporter stood from her chair. "Milton police tell me that the search for Bryce Pearson has been reignited with this additional information. The Pearsons have engaged the assistance of second-term US Senator Hugh McMillan. The senator is believed to be working with his contacts in Washington to determine if there is any validity to the claims that government agents were involved in the disappearance of these five young people from the Milton area.

"Finally, in a curious twist, sources tell me that authorities are also questioning a respected computer science professor at Tech, Dr. William Hendrickson. While it's unknown what connection Dr. Hendrickson may have with the missing students, Tyler Barnes may have been associated with some of the department's research programs. Both Bryce and Maggie had applied to attend Tech as freshmen next fall. Time will tell what, if any, connection this all has to the missing students.

"Reporting live on location in Milton, this is Marsha Hoyle, Channel 6 News, on your side."

Zach stared at the fading image of his mom and dad before the station switched to the weather forecast. Seeing his parents so hopeless was more than he could take. He stood and walked into the hallway so the others wouldn't hear him cry.

He sat in the dark, against the wall in the next room, for a long time. The hurt floated in his brain, taunting him like a schoolyard bully. It was ridiculous to think they'd be able to make the pile of junk work together to open the bridge. Even though Bryce had seemed so close in the hologram, he was probably never coming back.

Even if Bryce did make it home, Zach might not be around to see him. His body was breaking down, he could feel it. Whatever had happened to him when crossing the bridge, or maybe from being in the virtual world, it was slowly wearing him down. He'd keep a brave face for the others, but Zach feared it was just a matter of time.

Eventually he stood and walked back to the main room. Everyone was sleeping, spread across the floor in their sleeping bags. Tyler was slumped over at the computer, his head in his arms. Zach yawned and slid into his sleeping bag. He pushed it a little closer to Maggie's sleeping bag and closed his eyes.

Maybe when he woke, it would all be different. This would all be just a dream. Bryce and he would both be home sleeping in their own beds with Mom and Dad down the hall. Life would make sense again. He smiled to himself at the thought and drifted off.

* * *

Zach woke up suddenly. He'd been dreaming again. It was the same nightmare he'd had every night since he'd crossed the bridge. Yao was staring at him through the video monitor next to the JOSHUA machine. The Ranger's hand was shoving him toward the curling green smoke in the chamber. And then he'd wake up.

Zach turned his head and realized that he'd pushed up against Maggie's sleeping bag. Her arm was draped over his chest in her sleep. He gently lifted her arm and slipped out of his warm cocoon. He shivered at the cool air in the room. Someone had forgotten to turn on the space heater. The cold seemed to seep through the aged cement block walls. He tiptoed around the sleeping bags to the heater, twisting the dial until an orange glow filled the coils.

He had to pee, so he grabbed one of Charlie's flashlights from the worktable and slinked out of the room. He peered into the dilapidated bathroom they'd been using up the hall. It seemed even creepier in the middle of the night— cobwebs lined the edge of the ceiling and the old tiles were caked with layers of dirt. An unpainted area above the sink formed a gray rectangle where a mirror used to hang. Maggie and Jess had refused to go in the bathroom at first, but as the reality of their situation sank in, they'd agreed to use it after giving the toilet seat a hearty scrub.

When he finished, Zach came back down the hall, suddenly feeling awake. He passed their room and walked to the back entrance with the broken window. He nearly bumped the tripwire, but remembered it at the last minute and carefully navigated around it. He followed the nylon fishing line to the side of the room where it connected to the bell.

As he focused his flashlight beam on the rusted metal bell, a glint caught his eye. The silky wire had moved, but it wasn't ringing the bell. He leaned closer and realized the thin tip of the metal striker had rusted off, preventing it from reaching the side of the bell.

Zach placed his finger on the line and felt a gentle tug, like a nibbling on his worm at the fishing pond behind the VFW. He looked over his shoulder to the opening beneath the boarded window just as the line surged forward, yanking the bell straight past his grip and onto the floor.

He snapped his head back to the window. His heart was pounding. Something big had hit the trip wire. Someone was coming. He knew he needed to warn the others, but then two things happened simultaneously. A burning sensation returned to his leg, signaling the start of another episode. And he heard a scraping from above the window as someone pulled back the board.

There was no time to run. He fought back the pain as a foot dangled through the window. He had to do something.

He blinked his eyes, trying to stay alert as the sensation crept up his side. He spied a two-by-four propped against the cinderblocks. He lifted the board and cocked it behind his ear like a baseball bat. As the figure landed on the cement floor, Zach let the wood fly, striking the intruder on the forehead and sending them to the ground in a heap.

Then the pain overwhelmed him. Zach collapsed, landing on the floor next to the intruder. He recognized the face of the person lying on the cement just before he blacked out.

Oh, no. What had he done?

CHAPTER TWENTY-SIX_

W hen Zach opened his eyes, he was back in his sleeping bag. He blinked and rubbed a dull ache that still hummed with energy on the side of his head where his hair had whitened. As he sat, the memory of the night flooded back. The others were huddled on the far side of the room, talking excitedly. He looked past Jess and Tyler to see Maggie wrapping a gauze bandage around a man's head.

Zach closed his eyes again, remembering how he'd swung the board at the figure climbing through the window.

It was Professor Hendrickson.

"You okay, man?" asked Andrew, moving over to him.

Zach covered his face with his palm. "Is he okay?"

Andrew nodded. "Looks like you clocked him pretty solid, though. Maggie found you both ten minutes ago when she got up to use the bathroom and saw your empty sleeping bag. She woke us all up to find you, but we're not sure how long the two of you were lying there. Jess found a first-aid kit down the hall. Maggie's using it to bandage Hendrickson's forehead. He lost some blood, but we think he'll be okay."

"I need to go over there," said Zach, standing from his sleeping bag. He crossed the room and crouched in front of the professor. "Are you okay?"

"Other than feeling like I went ten rounds with Evander Holyfield," Professor Hendrickson replied.

"I'm really sorry," Zach muttered. "I thought you were a guard or something."

"It's okay. I shouldn't have surprised you all, but I thought coming under the cover of darkness was my best way to get in undetected."

Andrew chuckled. "It takes a lot to sneak past Zach, here."

Maggie finished with the bandage and looked back at Zach. "What happened?"

Zach explained how he'd gone to the bathroom and then saw the trip line pull. "The bell was broken, so it didn't ring. Then I started to… I had another episode. I grabbed the board and smacked him just before I blacked out."

Professor Hendrickson looked back at him. "Episode?"

"He's been having them more and more," said Tyler. "I think it's either connected to his reentry or the ongoing disturbances we have been seeing."

The professor's expression turned serious. "How long has this been happening?"

Zach sighed, realizing there was no point in hiding

anything. "A while. It was infrequent at first, every couple of weeks, but since they took me to the hospital in Quantico, the episodes have been coming more often, and they hurt a lot worse than before."

The professor stared Zach in the eye. "I need you to tell me every time it happens from now on, do you understand? This could be serious."

Zach nodded. "Okay."

"What are you doing here, anyway, Professor?" asked Charlie.

"We saw you on the news," added Andrew. "Are you on the run, too?"

He looked over at Tyler questioningly. "You didn't tell them?"

"Not exactly," Tyler answered, shaking his head.

"Tell us what, Ty?" said Jess.

"I reached out to the professor yesterday after talking with Bryce again while you guys were in the lab. I'm worried that he hasn't cracked the activation codes yet. Since the heat is coming down on the professor from the Feds, I thought it might motivate him to join our rogue band of misfits. We could certainly use the extra brainpower, but I didn't want to get your hopes up until he got here." Tyler turned to Zach. "Sorry, I should have told you."

"General Weber was not pleased with your caper, breaking Zach out of the facility," said Hendrickson. "Not to mention finding Heather Avanair's body in the garage."

"We didn't kill her, I swear," exclaimed Charlie. "Someone drove by and just started firing."

"Of course you didn't," Hendrickson replied. "Tyler already explained to me what happened."

"Do you know who killed her?" asked Zach.

"Not officially, but I have my suspicions," said the professor. "It certainly wasn't us. She was of great value. The government was hoping to extract important information from her. There's only one person who'd have wanted her quiet."

"Yao," muttered Charlie.

Hendrickson nodded. "That's my guess."

Andrew carried over an oversized black duffel bag and dropped it at Hendrickson's feet. "I'd say you were planning to stay a while, but this is too heavy to be clothes and a pillow."

"I come bearing gifts." The professor smiled and unzipped the bag. "I made one last visit to the lab in the cavern before General Weber revoked my security clearance." He pulled out a square device that looked like an external hard drive. "This is a sequenced encryption decoder. It should be able to identify the activation codes. It might take a few hours, but I think we'll find them."

"Awesome," said Tyler, taking the decoder. "I'll hook this up and let Bryce know."

Zach looked at the bag. It was still bulging. "What else do you have in there?"

The professor pulled out a round, black disc.

"A new sensor!" exclaimed Charlie. "Where did you get that?"

"Another item I liberated from the cavern. I don't think anyone will miss it."

Charlie turned to Tyler. "You knew about all this?"

"I didn't want to freak you guys out," he replied, "but we were never going to receive the bridge transmission with a broken sensor. We need at least three to form the net."

Charlie looked over at Maggie and Zach and winked. "I present to you, Plan B."

They laughed, and Zach felt a glimmer of hope creep back into his mind.

"You're a lifesaver, Professor," said Jess.

Hendrickson smiled. "I'm glad we're all in this together now. But I'm afraid our work is just beginning." He turned to Tyler. "Can you pull Bryce back online? I need to share some things with all of you."

Andrew groaned. "That doesn't sound good."

Charlie showed Professor Hendrickson to the bathroom and got him some food and water while Tyler worked to communicate with Bryce inside *Kingdom*. Soon the flickering light of Bryce's hologram shined out into the room. He greeted Hendrickson and listened as Tyler updated him on the decoding device and the news of the new coordinate sensor.

"But the professor wants to update us all on something," said Tyler, turning around as they all looked at Hendrickson with anticipation.

"As you know," Professor Hendrickson began, "General Weber has commandeered the entire JOSHUA project. Even before he revoked my clearance yesterday, I could tell he was pushing me further onto the periphery. Something big was happening."

"We knew about the abnormal readings," said Tyler. "Has it gotten worse?"

The professor gathered his thoughts before continuing. "The military has intercepted communications from China that indicate Yao is on the verge of finalizing a major scientific discovery. It could dwarf what he was doing with Eden. Combined with the cosmic abnormalities, it's put the military on full alert. It seems that Bryce is right—Fitz is constructing a stronger, portable bridge communicator for Yao."

"So maybe General Weber will help us open the bridge to get Bryce home," said Zach.

"It might not be that easy, I'm afraid," Hendrickson replied. "While bringing Bryce home is the foremost objective for all of us, the general is looking at a much bigger scope. He fears that any reopening of the bridge might severely damage the cosmic balance, possibly creating an irrevocable tear between dimensions."

"Which would be bad?" asked Andrew.

Hendrickson raised his eyebrows. "Very."

"What's the general going to do?" asked Jess.

"While I can't be certain," Hendrickson answered slowly, "I believe he's preparing a catastrophic charge to send back through the portal to destroy the bridge and prevent any further transmissions."

Andrew gasped. "Nukes!" He looked around the group, dumbfounded. "I was right..."

"But what about Bryce?" Zach stared at his brother's flickering face. He didn't want to think about Bryce being killed by a giant mushroom cloud sent across to destroy the virtual world. "We can't just leave him there!"

"Zach," Bryce called out through the hologram. "Let him finish."

"Of course not," said the professor. "To be honest, that's the main reason I'm here. Weber and his team don't understand what they're dealing with. We obviously can't allow them to detonate the bridge. The repercussions of such an explosion could be far more damaging to the cosmic fabric than anything that Yao might initiate. Weber is responding how generals do, through a brute display of force."

"Except this isn't a standard enemy," muttered Jess.

"Exactly," said Hendrickson. "The solution, if there is one, will lie in science, not in military might."

"Okay," said Charlie, "so what's next? Can we still activate the bridge at the water tower without, like, you know, screwing up the universe?"

Hendrickson nodded. "Our hope is to bring Bryce back across and quickly close down the transmission stream. Permanently, if possible."

"I like the sound of that," said Bryce.

"If everything goes according to plan," said Tyler, "we should be able to decode the activation sequence this morning. Bryce can then load it into the mainframe while we pack up here and drive to Milton. Then we'll position the sensors and set up the equipment at the water tower."

"Is that all?" Maggie asked, nervously.

"Easy-peasy," said Charlie, grinning. "What could go wrong?"

Nervous laughter filled the room as they considered the risky plan. Zach stepped next to the hologram. "Be careful, Bryce."

Bryce waved back confidently. "I'll see you really soon, little brother."

Maggie gripped Zach's hand and smiled at Bryce's image. "I love you. Promise you'll come back to me."

Bryce smiled at her as his image faded. "I promise."

CHAPTER TWENTY-SEVEN

Yao stared so long at the sparkling water, he nearly toppled in. The pool glowed green from the colored lights he'd had installed along the sides. They looked like runway lights at the airport. Which was appropriate, Yao thought, for he would be taking off, vaulting from this crumbling rock to his new existence. His decaying body would be transported to a new, permanent kingdom, where he would wield supreme authority. *His* kingdom had been designed by an entire secret team of programmers in Shanghai. It would be far greater than the pathetic video game world they'd developed to feed the hunger of the feeble-minded youth.

Mr. Sturgis had first presented the clever idea of building the portal under the guise of a rooftop swimming pool. Something much simpler would have easily sufficed, but unlike his remaining days, money was not in short supply. The walls of the rooftop natatorium were made from the strongest glass available, built to withstand hurricane-force gusts. The roof was the same material, but featured a retractable, circular opening in the center. When the powerful beam shot from the heavens to transport him to paradise, it would pass through the opening and into the center of the pool which stretched thirty feet to the bottom. It was possible that the energy beam might completely obliterate the building, but that was of little concern for Yao. He would already have been whisked into another dimension, ready to begin his new eternity.

The thought brought a thin smile to his lips but sent him into a painful, dry cough. He touched the tender area just below his chin and then pulled up a clear mask connected to an oxygen tank that had been wheeled next to him at the water's edge. Yao nodded to Sturgis across the pool, where the Swede waited for the signal to start their afternoon status briefing.

Yao wondered if Sturgis expected to join him on the journey, or if he'd even want to. They'd built their relationship on the fine line between power and trust. The thought flashed through Yao's mind that all Sturgis needed was one quick kick to the oxygen tank which would drag Yao down to the depths of the pool and, in an instant, deprive him of all that he'd worked for. But there had been many opportunities for Sturgis to challenge Yao's authority in the past, and he had remained faithful.

No, the path was now clear. If Mr. Fitz was to be

believed from his isolated Canadian workstation, the plan to open the bridge would begin in a matter of hours.

Sturgis reached Yao's side of the pool and wheeled the old man's oxygen tank toward a table and two cushioned chairs. Yao eased into the padded fabric slowly, sucking deeply from the oxygen before sliding the mask from his mouth. While his mind remained razor sharp, speaking had recently become more difficult. He motioned for Sturgis to begin.

"Thank you, sir," Sturgis said. "First, Mr. Fitz has relayed that the system is fully programmed and ready to go. We remain on schedule to activate the bridge and initiate transmission before first light at four AM."

"Excellent," said Yao. They'd arranged that the bridge would open while most of Shanghai was still asleep. In his head he played out the scene to come—servants would assist him into the water, floating him to a specially crafted platform between the opening in the roof and the thirty-foot depths. By the time the city awoke, he'd be gone.

"I'm pleased to report that Mr. Cox has successfully met with Dr. Avanair," Sturgis continued. "She will not present a problem moving forward."

Yao nodded his approval, although it was a pity they'd had to resort to such deadly measures for a woman whose great beauty was matched by her intelligence. There had been a point when he'd thought about bringing her on the journey as a worthy companion to meet his needs. But it had been a fleeting thought. Why bother with having to keep someone else happy? A virtual harem would be much more controllable.

He caught a slight hesitation in Sturgis's voice. "While his mission was a success, Mr. Cox also reports that Ms. Avanair was exiting the facility when they met. She was with some of the troublesome young people, Bryce Pearson's brother, Zach, and…" Sturgis shifted uncomfortably in his seat. "Charles Kilroy."

Yao raised the bare skin above his eyes that his brows had once occupied at the mention of Mr. Kilroy. He broke into a long cough and quickly pulled the oxygen mask over his mouth. Those kids continued to be a thorn in his side. But that, too, would soon not matter. He drew a measured breath and slowly formed the words in his throat until they fell from his lips. "And the other?"

Sturgis nodded. "The Ranger has been dispatched within *Kingdom's* world. He'll be approaching his target shortly. I have no doubt he will soon eradicate that problem as well." He nodded uneasily at the glimmering water. "It's late, sir. You should get some rest. You have a long journey ahead of you."

Yao grunted and took several long draws of the oxygen. Young Bryce was the one wild card that still presented him with a flicker of concern. The boy was a nuisance, but he had a resourceful mind. It was highly unlikely he could create meaningful interference from within the virtual world; however, Yao had underestimated the boy before, and he prided himself on not making the same mistake twice.

Yao raised his eyes to the retractable circle in the roof and pictured what lay beyond the darkened night sky. He had to hold on for just a few hours more. It was nearly time.

CHAPTER TWENTY-EIGHT_

T he roar of engines broke the silence of the woods. Three tan Humvees skidded to a stop around the perimeter fence. A team of soldiers panned out, surrounding the complex. At the signal of the thick man with the graying buzz cut, the first group burst through the main entrance, storming down a long hallway and through an unsecured fire door. The second group pulled back a square sheet of plywood and slid through a broken window frame.

The clatter of combat boots marching over concrete echoed through the hall passages as both teams moved toward the dark, inner center of the abandoned annex building. Strong flashlight beams cut past the cobwebs and layers of dust, scanning room by room, methodically checking for signs of movement.

But everything was still.

The only signs that the space had been recently occupied were spare electronic equipment scattered across a worktable along the wall, two empty water jugs, and a trash bin stuffed with food wrappers and cans.

"Sector secure, General," the team leader spoke into his radio mic at his collar.

"What's the report?" a gruff voice answered back.

"It's empty, sir. There's no one here."

General Weber threw his radio onto the seat of the nearest vehicle and cursed.

* * *

THE EXPLORER PARKED NEXT to Hendrickson's black truck on the edge of the clearing in front of the water tower. Zach's stomach had been tied in knots the whole trip. He'd worried a police barricade was going to be waiting at every turn, blocking their journey. But Charlie seemed to be right. No one suspected they'd return to Milton. Zach longed to stop by his house, to comfort his parents and tell them he was okay, but he knew there would be time for that at the end. He and Bryce would do it together.

They'd stuffed the two vehicles with all kinds of equipment from the compound—two long, folding tables, a couple of computer terminals and monitors, the coordinate sensors, and what seemed like miles of thick black cable. It had taken three trips to get it to the vehicles in the woods, but they would need it all to connect the systems to the power substation fifty yards past the water tower. Charlie had seen the electrical boxes when he'd first waited for Bryce at the tower. The substation also served as the source for a fiber optic cable that ran from the main road to the neighborhood on the other side of the woods. The borrowed juice would power the transmission perfectly. It might black out the rest of town, but they could apologize later.

Tyler checked the time. "We have two hours to set up. Bryce is pushing the activation code at exactly four o'clock. By that time, we need to have run the cables, connected with the power box, set up the computers, and most importantly, placed the sensors up there." He pointed to the top of the water basin.

Zach craned his neck to glimpse the top of the hulking tower above them. He'd heard guys at school talk about this place, but he had never seen it in person. He'd been locked up when the others came and met with Charlie. It was hard to visualize how the rusting structure could connect the bridge to *Kingdom*, but things had stopped making sense a long time ago. He trusted that Bryce, Tyler, and Charlie knew what they were doing, and it made him even more confident having Professor Hendrickson on their side.

"Who's gonna do that?" Andrew asked warily. "I'm not great with heights."

Jess shook her head. "What a shocker."

A metal ladder rose to a platform that ran along the bottom portion of the water tank. But getting from the platform to the roof of the basin would be a harrowing climb. A series of thin metal bars led along the side of the tank to the top. Zach would have a tough time handling those heights on a good day, but he knew it would be foolish to volunteer now, given his spells.

"I'll do it," said Charlie. "I don't mind heights."

"We'll probably need someone else to help you get the cables up to the platform and around the basin," said Hendrickson.

"I'll help," said Maggie. "I've been on the platform before with Bryce. It's not so bad once you're up there."

"Great," the professor said. "Tyler, why don't you assemble the sensors and cables on the ground here so they're ready to take up. I'll start working on splicing into the power station."

Charlie directed the rest of them where to place the folding tables to serve as a central command center for the computers. They needed to be far enough away from the tower so that the energy burst from the transmission stream wouldn't overwhelm the equipment, but close enough to be able to react to anything that might go wrong.

CHAPTER TWENTY-NINE_

B ryce had always been confident before big events.
Many of his track teammates battled serious butter-
flies before meets. Some even regularly vomited before the
starting gun fired. But he'd had a quiet calm, just like before
a big exam. He'd always had the ability and the will to
succeed, but what he faced now was on a whole other level.
This wasn't a game. Or even a test. His life was on the line,
and there was no restart.

He trusted the plan he'd developed with Tyler, Charlie,
and now Professor Hendrickson, but there were still so
many things that could go wrong. Hendrickson's device
appeared to have cracked the activation codes, but much of
their plan rested on Fitz's new programming sequences.
The fat man's hologram had curiously disappeared earlier
that morning. Was he finished? Had he detected Bryce's
pilfering? For all they knew, Fitz could have leaked Bryce
corrupted code to throw him off. There hadn't been time

to check every line, so Bryce had needed to trust Fitz's work.

But it was too late to change anything now. They were racing against time. If Fitz helped Yao open the bridge first, there was no telling what would happen. And Bryce couldn't stay here much longer. The drastic climate change outside the cave was just the latest evidence that something bad was happening inside *Kingdom*. It was like the world was crumbling around him. He couldn't be there when it all fell apart. He had to get home.

Bryce checked the time. He'd programmed a computer to show the hour and minute back in Milton, since he'd realized that time operated at a much faster speed inside *Kingdom*. He thought of it like two spinning wheels, a ring of smaller circumference inside a larger one. A single rotation of the outer ring would take longer than the smaller, inner ring. Bryce was on the inner ring, inside the virtual world. His days came and went much faster than the longer rotation of the real world's outer ring.

Even so, the others should have arrived at the water tower and set up the positioning equipment by now. In his last communication with Tyler, they'd agreed that Bryce would begin the bridge's activation sequence at 4:00 PM in Milton's time. Still thirty minutes of real time to wait. Everything was ready, but thinking about it made him antsy.

He glanced back toward the elevator, suddenly filled with an urge for one last peek outside. The virtual world had never been home, but he'd been there for so long. Had the atmosphere continued to deteriorate since he'd last taken the elevator to the surface, or had he witnessed an isolated weather event, like the rapidly changing weather patterns on the Central Plateau?

He decided to check once more. He could ensure that the elevator shaft was still working, since it would serve as his exit portal. He glanced back at the monitors and then moved to the elevator. Being in the small space reminded him of huddling together with Rachel in the Eden machine's chamber. It had all happened so suddenly. In a flash they'd been thrust across the bridge through time and space to the grain silo. It seemed a lifetime ago.

Bryce pushed the button to the surface. But as the doors closed shut, his mind flooded with second thoughts. What if the atmosphere had turned toxic and he passed out when he reached the surface? Then he'd never be able to activate the bridge on time.

He lunged for the controls, but the elevator had only the single button. There was no emergency stop. Bryce stared at the polished metal door as the car ascended through the narrow shaft in the cave rock. He braced himself for the surface.

The elevator stopped with a jerk. For a moment, Bryce thought something had gone wrong. Being stuck in the shaft would doom him just as much as any poison gas. But then the door gently slid open, revealing the surface.

The heat hit him like a slap across the face. The temperature had risen dramatically, searing him like he'd stepped into an oven. Clouds piled against each other in the darkened sky like crumpled vehicles in a massive accident on the interstate. The clouds glowed in iridescent green, purple, and orange. Furious bolts of lightning danced at the horizon, crashing to the ground in a constant energy display, like a Tesla coil at the science museum. Wind whipped around the side of the mountain and pushed at him from the left. He pulled his shirt over his nose and mouth, but the sulfur taste was stronger and was already burning his lungs. It was like the world was breaking apart.

Bryce spied the log he'd used to hold the door. But as he stretched down to the ground for the wood, a powerful blast threw him forward. The log splintered apart. He fell to the ground outside the elevator door.

Still dazed by the sudden blast, Bryce looked back at the elevator. If the door closed, it would trap him on the surface. He kicked his leg into the doorway. The metal pounded into his leg, tightening against the still tender spot where the razor wire had cut his calf. He screamed in pain, but the door remained open.

He tried to get his bearings. What had happened? Had he almost been hit by a lightning bolt? He squinted through the wind-driven dust across the dark landscape. A blurred form moved swiftly through the field. It was a Ranger, striding toward Bryce through the shadows. His hulking gun was aimed and ready to fire again.

Bryce spun around and tried to move further into the elevator, but the door seemed stuck, clamped onto his leg like a vice. He slid against the frame, but as he rose from the ground, a rock exploded just inches from his head. Gunfire boomed against the mountain. He dropped back to the ground as rocks and dirt rained onto his head. He was pinned down.

Bryce cursed at himself for coming back up. What was he thinking? He strained at the door with his hands while using his free leg to push against the rock for leverage. Gradually, the pressure released and he slid back into the elevator.

He looked back outside. The Ranger was running now, his weapon raised again to fire. Bryce desperately pressed the control button, but as the door slid closed, another round exploded. The car rocked back against the rear of the elevator shaft. The ceiling light shattered.

Bryce braced himself against the wall in the darkness, praying that the elevator would move. The Ranger was too close. Another direct hit from the gun would plunge him violently through the mountain.

Time seemed to stand still as he waited for the elevator to move. Finally, it began a slow descent back toward the lab. Bryce wiped sweat mixed with gravel and dirt from his face. His breath came in spurts from the thick, noxious air and his close escape.

When he sensed he was nearly at the bottom, the elevator suddenly dropped into a free-fall. The car banged and scraped against the metal of the shaft like a car bouncing off a median. It thudded to a stop, stuck at an odd angle in the shaft. Was he back at the lab, or some-where in between?

Bryce dug his fingers into the edge of the door and

tugged it open. The metal inched back, revealing a sliver of light. A foot-wide space opened along the elevator car floor, revealing a light. He stuck his head through and saw the ceiling of the lab. He hadn't made it all the way down, but he could slide through the opening. He flattened his body and fell the few remaining feet to the lab's cement floor. He collapsed and sucked in the clean air.

Was the Ranger able to open the outer door on the side of the mountain? Would he blast his way in? Bryce stared at the damaged elevator shaft. It would never work as his exit portal now. A whole squadron of Rangers might be descending toward him, and he couldn't risk that the damage to the shaft would prevent the bridge from working. He had to use something else.

He thought back to his conversation with the others. He'd nearly suggested the pool on the other side of the lab beyond the waterfall. Now it might be his only option, regardless of whatever creatures lurked in its waters. He'd have to act fast. He climbed back into the elevator shaft and disconnected the cables and the coordinate sensors he'd positioned along the bottom. He gathered them in his arms and carried them out the other side of the lab toward the pool.

Bryce stepped through the gentle falling water. Light already filled the cavern. Millions of tiny glowing organisms churned and bubbled through the water, as if foreseeing a coming event. He scanned the surface for larger movement, but there was no sign of the creature. He shuddered at the memory of its sharp teeth bearing down on him.

Bryce pulled the cables into a folded circle like a giant lasso. He grasped a cleft in the rock wall for balance and then heaved the cable and two of the sensors into the center of the pool. He held on to the cable's back edge and the third sensor, releasing it at the last moment so it would open up into a wide ring. The cables smacked along the water's surface, the three sensors briefly floating like round buoys. They appeared to stay in the open lasso shape even as they sank slowly beneath the surface.

He pushed off on the rock and spun back through the waterfall, following the lead cable back to the lab. Electronics in the virtual world seemed to operate through water and without a power source, but he'd still need to have the sensors connected to the mainframe.

As he reached his workstation, a boom exploded from high up the elevator shaft. The Ranger must have penetrated the mountain's outer door. Were the others ready at the water tower to receive the transmission? He checked his Milton clock. There were still fifteen minutes until he was to activate the bridge. The Ranger would be on top of him any second. He couldn't wait that long.

Bryce stared at the monitor and tried to push back his panic and clear his mind. He had to alter the coding sequences so that the coordinate sensors matched their new location in the pool. He scrolled through the directories in a flash, quickly identifying the right code. He punched feverishly at the keyboard, relying on his years of practice to readjust the sequences faster than he'd ever done before.

With the last update, he banged the enter key emphatically. He stared up as the activation sequence streamed across the monitor. Five minutes. It was the shortest he could set the countdown and still give the quantum accelerators enough energy to open the bridge.

His mind flashed back to the Eden machine and how Charlie had sat at the mainframe, while Bryce had run with Rachel into the chamber as the green mist rose all around them, and how they could only watch as Q2 guards had stormed the room and gunned Charlie down. It seemed like yesterday, but also years ago.

A heavy thud sounded from the elevator shaft. Combat boots landing on the top of the elevator car. The Ranger was here.

Bryce took a final glance at the screen, synching the countdown in his brain. Four minutes. He scanned the lab for somewhere to hide. He'd be an easy target standing by the waterfall. Treading water in the pool might only result in an early meal for the creature. He ran to the controls on the wall and lowered the overhead lights to their dimmest setting. The air filled with the loud humming he'd heard from the caves on his arrival. He'd have to hide in the shadows. Anything to avoid detection just for a few precious minutes.

Bryce crept beside some shelves on the side of the lab nearest the exit and mapped out a sprint to the pool. Metal scraped as the Ranger ripped an opening in the elevator shaft. He jumped down into the lab, the sound of his boots echoing as they hit the cement floor. Bryce pressed his shoulder blades against the wall behind the shelves and held his breath. The heavy footsteps clomped closer.

Did the Ranger know about the bridge countdown, or was this just an avatar on a simple search-and-destroy mission with Bryce as his sole target? Despite his fear, Bryce tried to concentrate. He couldn't lose track of the time. Two minutes. At least he thought so.

A long shadow fell across the floor. The Ranger was too close. He'd see Bryce at any second. Bryce had to move.

He slowly crawled between the tables, toward the hallway to the waterfall. But his leg bumped a shelf. A tin canister fell to the cement. The Ranger spun on its heel at the sound. Bryce peeked over a table. They made eye contact, and the gun quickly rose.

Bryce dove to the floor as the Ranger fired. The table exploded into pieces. This was crazy. He was never going to make it with the Ranger firing that gun. There was still at least a minute on the countdown. He had to buy more time.

Bryce leapt behind another table, moving purposefully away from the computer workstation. If the Ranger damaged the controls, he'd never be able to activate the bridge. The Ranger clipped off another series of thundering shots that were deafening in the indoor space. Splinters of wood and metal pelted Bryce's body as he fell back to the floor. Bright splotches of red dripped from his forehead onto the cement as he struggled to catch his breath.

The sight of the blood triggered a memory—he was by the pond with Rachel. The Ranger had looked like a fisherman. Bryce had walloped the big man across the head with the boat oar.

Bryce grabbed a chunk of wood from the lab floor and lobbed it across the room toward the elevator like a grenade. When the Ranger pivoted toward the sound, Bryce picked up the leg from a metal stool. He gripped it tightly and rose to his feet. He lunged forward, slamming the bar into the back of the distracted Ranger's head. The man remained on his feet, but he was knocked off balance. His heavy weapon flew from his hands and slid out of sight beneath a table.

Now was Bryce's chance.

The Ranger screamed in anger as Bryce turned and dashed toward the exit. He'd lost track of the countdown in his head, but it had to be close to time.

He risked a glance over his shoulder. The Ranger's enormous strides had quickly cut the distance. He was only steps behind. The Ranger's hand stretched out at the waterfall. His fingers dug into Bryce's shoulder as he leaped into the air.

But he was already flying—soaring through the waterfall like it was his backyard sprinkler on a hot summer day. As he burst into the cavern, the world seemed to slow. The light across the pool was blinding as the organisms whirled like a synchronized aquatic ballet.

In midair, he spotted the fin. It surged toward him through the water. The creature's head rose to the surface. Its massive teeth-filled mouth opened wide.

Suddenly the coordinate sensors clicked on, shining in a brilliant green ring below him in the water. An enormous beam of energy shot from inside the ring. It blasted from the depths and straight through the rock dome of the cavern ceiling.

Bryce could almost count the monster's teeth. He could nearly feel the Ranger's breath on his neck behind him. But as Bryce touched the water, the great beam of energy enveloped him. He was blinded by the light. Everything else washed away. The cavern disappeared. A long tunnel of light stretched out ahead of him as his body was transported.

It was happening. He was going home.

But was it too soon? Were they ready for him on the other side?

CHAPTER THIRTY

Zach watched from the ground as Charlie scaled the metal footholds along the side of the water basin. The coordinate sensor cable was draped around his neck so he could grasp the rungs with both hands. The distance from the bottom of the tank to the roof didn't look too far—Andrew thought it was about twenty feet—but Zach's stomach turned just watching. Maggie stood on the platform that circled the base of the water tank. She fed Charlie lengths of cable as he climbed higher.

Professor Hendrickson had successfully penetrated the power utility substation, splicing cables into both the power source and the fiber optic Internet line. The connection ran the two computers, which Tyler and Jess operated on the command center table, and the cable that dangled from the side of the water tower. Tyler turned a monitor toward the clearing to show the time left until the bridge transmission.

Just forty-five minutes.

Zach pictured Bryce completing his own preparations in the underground lab. Was he scared, or was he the same confident person he'd always been? Had the virtual world worn at his body like it was eating at Zach's? Would Zach ever be able to shake the debilitating episodes that kept hitting him like a truck? There was no point thinking too far ahead. First, they had to get Bryce back. They could deal with the rest later.

"Is it just me, or is the sky getting darker?" asked Andrew, pointing behind them up the trail to the main road.

Zach turned and saw a towering cloud bank forming on the horizon. Thunderstorms often rolled through Milton during the humid days of summer, but never this time of year. They all stared as the formations thickened and grew, taking on an otherworldly green tint. "I've seen this before," Zach muttered.

"You have?" asked Andrew.

Zack nodded. "When I was inside *Kingdom*, before the bridge opened at the chasm." He stared up at Charlie as he reached the basin roof. "It's going to work. I can feel it."

As Zach uttered the words, a gust of wind swept across the valley. It pushed at Charlie up on the water basin, and his foot slipped off the top rung of the ladder. His body swung into the air as he clung to the roof edge with his hands.

"Oh, my god!" Jess exclaimed. "Charlie!"

The cable fell from around Charlie's neck, but caught on his ankle and flapped around his leg in the breeze. He

214

pulled his chest onto the roof, but when he raised his knee to swing his leg over, the cable caught and pulled him back. He was dangling a hundred feet in the air.

"Hold on, Charlie!" Maggie shouted below him from the platform. "I'm coming."

"The sensor's catching on that rung below him," said Andrew.

Zach saw he was right, but there was nothing they could do from the ground as Maggie began a desperate climb up the basin to loosen the cable. The sky seemed to grow darker with each rung she passed, as though it was angry and determined to blow them both into the treetops.

When Maggie reached the twisted sensor cable, she grasped a metal rung with one hand while leaning out and tugging at the cable with the other. Everyone on the ground watched in frozen horror as she worked at the cable. Charlie still dangled from the edge. With each gust of wind, his legs flailed out into the open air. The sensor was jammed between the rung and the basin, but a final hard tug from Maggie freed it.

"I think she's got it!" said Andrew.

Maggie shouted up to Charlie and he swung his leg up over the edge and collapsed onto the roof. Zach exhaled in relief as Maggie strained to pull enough slack into the cable so that Charlie could move it into position on the roof.

The wind was whipping now. Charlie inched along in a crouch, dragging the cable with one hand while anchoring himself with his other to keep from blowing off the roof. They watched him place the first sensor on the near side, attaching it with plastic zip ties to keep it in place. Then he inched his way toward the two back points of the roof that were out of their sight from the ground.

"How much time?" Jess called back to Tyler.

"Thirty minutes. I think we'll be good, as long as he doesn't fall."

"Don't say that," Andrew muttered.

Professor Hendrickson looked up from the computers. "Once Charlie positions the sensors and they're both off the tower, someone will need to throw the breaker lever." He pointed to the substation through the woods.

"I'll do it," said Zach. He hated just standing there watching. If he couldn't climb the tower or do anything important to help, the least he could do was throw the power switch. Hendrickson had shown him where it was when they'd first dragged the cables to the substation.

Hendrickson watched the unnatural clouds above them. "Amazing."

"It's like the atmosphere can sense the cosmic occurrence," said Tyler. "Just like those readings you talked about."

"Our world, I'm afraid, is not designed to withstand prolonged tears in the dimensional fabric," Hendrickson yelled over the wind. "It was one of our concerns when we first conceived the idea for the JOSHUA project years ago." He shook his head. "It was a journey that we should never have embarked upon. I see now that the risks are far too great."

As if in agreement, a clap of thunder sounded in the

distance. The professor stared back up at Charlie and Maggie. "We need to get them off that tower. This will get ugly fast."

"They've almost got it," said Zach.

Andrew pointed to the side of the roof. "There he is!" Charlie's head poked around the back of the peaked roof and into view. "He did it."

"Get over to the breaker, Zach. Once they're down, let's power it up. I want to make sure we have a solid connection." Professor Hendrickson waved his arms and shouted up to Maggie. "Come on down if you're ready!"

Zach stepped toward the woods, his head still tilted back to watch Charlie climb over the edge of the basin toward Maggie. He finally relaxed a bit when they both reached the platform and were climbing down the metal ladder. Then he turned and ran to the breaker box through the trees. They were almost there.

As he reached the power substation, the loud rotors of a helicopter suddenly buzzed just above the tree line—it was a military chopper. More motors roared behind him near the tower. Tires skidded in the dirt. Voices were yelling.

Zach spun around and sprinted back toward the others. He jumped behind a wide tree just before the clearing. His heart stopped when he peered out at the scene. A cloud of dust surrounded three tan Humvees parked in front of their makeshift command center. A dozen soldiers circled the others with their guns drawn. General Weber stepped from one of the vehicles and walked up to Professor Hendrickson.

Zach closed his eyes. Please, God, not now. They were so close!

The general was screaming and cursing at Hendrickson like he was about to combust. Two other soldiers motioned for Charlie and Maggie to finish coming down the last few rungs of the ladder.

Zach felt frozen behind the tree. No one had seen him, but what could he do? They couldn't abandon their plan now. Bryce was almost here. He was counting on them.

Zach glanced up at the water basin. Charlie seemed to have positioned the sensors around the roof. Everything was ready, but it wasn't time yet. Bryce wouldn't activate the transmission until the end of the countdown. Zach couldn't see the timer from where he hid, but there had to be at least fifteen minutes left. That was more than enough time for Weber to shut everything down.

Zach watched the soldiers march Maggie and Charlie over to the others. As they reached the tables, an enormous boom crashed across the sky. The general and all his men spun around, their weapons pointed above them. But then they slowly lowered their guns as they stared in awe at the scene above them.

A brilliant green fire burned through the clouds against the darkened sky. The military helicopter shook unsteadily and then peeled away. A piercing scream roared across the sky like it was ripping open. It was just like at the chasm.

The bridge was opening.

Zach didn't wait any longer. He turned and sprinted back to the power station. It was too early for the activation sequence, but it didn't matter. He knew that formation in the sky. For whatever reason, the bridge was opening early. He ducked through the hole they'd cut in the fence and opened the metal access door to the breaker panel. He pictured Bryce's face and said a silent prayer as he pulled the lever.

When Zach reached the clearing, even General Weber and his men stood motionless. Every head leaned back, all eyes transfixed and mouths agape, as they stared at the supernatural forces raging in the sky above them. Zach ran over and grabbed Maggie's arm. "I did it," he panted. "I turned on the power."

Maggie nodded and pointed at the sky. "It's happening."

Suddenly, a burst of energy streamed from a break in the clouds, coursing straight to the water tower. Everyone ducked and covered their ears as the beam connected with the coordinate sensors spread atop the basin. The rusted brown of the roof tiles shone a brilliant green. They seemed to expand in the light, which grew brighter and brighter until Zach finally had to shield his eyes.

Then, with a final surge of energy, the entire water basin groaned, sucking in toward itself before it exploded apart. A million gallons of water suddenly poured from the sky, thundering to the ground with the force of Niagara Falls.

"Grab hold of something!" shouted Professor Hendrickson, waving them into the woods. Everyone bolted for cover, clutching at the closest tree as the water surged like a dam break. The flood swept past the control center, overtaking the tables, computers, and all the equipment. It lifted the military vehicles off the ground and carried them down the sloping trail toward the road. The Explorer and Hendrickson's truck smashed together and wedged against the trees. General Weber and his soldiers hadn't made it to the woods. The water carried them across the clearing and out of sight down the trail. It was chaos.

Zach stared back at the metal frame of the tower. The green light of the energy beam reached straight to the ground. In a dynamic burst, it released a final blinding light.

And then it was gone.

CHAPTER THIRTY-ONE

Yao watched the roof sections symmetrically peel back to reveal the circular opening in the center. He'd never seen such fury in the night sky. The clouds had gathered as if at war against the very air in which they floated. They pounded into dense shapes and patterns lit by a thick, green, radiant energy that overwhelmed the normal light from the moon and the stars.

He waited, floating in his custom-made platform directly beneath the opening in the roof. He could almost feel the life draining from his frail body, but he reveled in knowing he had made it. After years of dreaming and building, his moment was at hand.

Sturgis relayed the countdown to speakers built into the platform from his position at the control panel in the corner of the room.

Thirty seconds.

Twenty.

Ten.

When the deafening roar pierced the sky, Yao closed his eyes. He envisioned himself reclined on a Persian chaise in his palace that overlooked the ocean, fanned by a dozen dark-haired virgins. All would be as he'd directed, his body no longer old and ravaged by disease but handsome, young and virile in his self-made paradise.

He looked up as a brilliant green beam streamed down through the roof. He felt his body becoming absorbed in the ray, dissolving as he transported to his new existence. It was as it was meant to be. He would be perfect.

He glanced down when he heard the shouting. Sturgis was racing along the pool's edge. He was yelling and fervently waving his hands. But Yao could not hear him over the scream of the energy pulsing through him. Whatever useless message the Swede had tried to communicate, it was too late.

Yao relaxed his body and smiled.

The bridge was open. He stared across an enormous highway of light, streaming like an ocean current toward the new dimension.

CHAPTER THIRTY-TWO

Zach strained to keep his left arm locked around the trunk of the tree, even as the bark peeled away beneath his fingers in the water flow. His right arm stretched toward Maggie, his hand locked onto her wrist as part of a human chain extending to Jess, Andrew, Tyler, and the professor. Charlie had scrambled higher and was hanging from a tree limb like a redheaded baboon.

As the current gradually subsided, draining into the forest in all directions, Zach steadied his feet on the ground and released his grip on the tree. He wiped his eyes and stared around the clearing. Sharp sections of sheet metal and wood lay scattered everywhere. It looked like they'd detonated a bomb. An upturned armored vehicle in the distance was the only evidence that General Weber and his men had ever been there.

"Are you all okay?" Professor Hendrickson called up the chain.

"I think so," Jess answered as they tried to balance in the soggy ground.

Zach turned back to where the water tower had stood. It looked like an industrial construction accident. The only parts of the tower that remained were the bottom sections of the support poles, but even they were bent and twisted like pretzels. What about the bridge? Had it opened? After all the destruction, had it even worked?

"Zach, look!" Maggie pointed into the mass of twisted steel. Something was clinging to a pole just off the ground. The object was partially covered by a gray section of sheet metal from the basin, but it looked like... a person!

Zach caught his breath.

It was Bryce.

Zach pushed off the tree trunk, running and sliding through the muddy ground toward the tower. Was it really him? Had it worked?

"Bryce!" Zach waved his arms, but didn't see any movement.

"Oh, God, is he hurt?" cried Maggie, following close behind.

As they approached, another section of metal pushed forward. It fell into the mud and a dark shadow emerged. Something else had crossed the bridge.

Zach and Maggie stopped in their tracks as a figure rose. The Sportsman stared at them with an evil grin.

"Zach, watch out!" called Andrew, as the man lunged toward them.

The Ranger's muscular hand grabbed Zach's shoulder. "Remember me?" he bellowed.

At the touch, pain shot through Zach's body. It poured from the Ranger's grip, surging straight to his toes. It felt like Zach had been charged with a million volts. His brain flashed through images of crossing the bridge, each one blinking in and out like a strobe light through his mind. He felt the life draining from his body as he faded out of consciousness.

Then suddenly the pressure lessened. The heavy grip released from Zach's shoulder. The Sportsman fell, splashing down into a deep puddle.

Zach glanced up. Bryce was lifting him up and carrying him away from the Ranger's reach. Zach met Bryce's eyes, so familiar, yet missing for so long. A smile flashed over his brother's lips as he nodded toward Maggie and the others.

But then Zach glanced back. The Ranger had regained his footing. He rose from the water, his face like a storm. He raised a powerful gun back in his hands.

There was a deafening clip of gunfire. It filled the air. Bryce lurched forward, hurling them both toward the cold ground. This couldn't be happening. Not again.

Zach looked back. General Weber's men were firing on the Sportsman from across the clearing. Then his head hit the ground and everything went dark.

CHAPTER THIRTY-THREE

Bryce pushed his hands against the muddy ground, struggling to raise his head. He sucked in a clean breath, the air fresh and clear, like he was inhaling it for the first time in his life.

"Oh, Bryce!" Maggie rushed at him, wrapping him in her arms and smothering him with kisses.

"Zach!" called Andrew.

"He's not moving," said Jess, circling around them.

Bryce turned and saw his brother lying face-down in a muddy puddle. He scooped him up in his arms. Zach's face was still, his eyes closed. Was he breathing? "Zach, come on buddy, wake up."

Maggie stood and waved to the soldiers who were now advancing on the fallen Ranger. "Somebody, help us!"

"General!" shouted Professor Hendrickson. "We need a medic for this boy!"

General Weber splashed over to them with two of his

men. "Clear a path!" he ordered, as one of the men kneeled to evaluate Zach.

The soldier looked up at General Weber. "We've got no pulse and he's not breathing. We need a defibrillator!"

Another soldier raced to the nearest Humvee as the medic began performing CPR, alternating between breathing into Zach's mouth and pushing with both hands on his chest.

Bryce knelt at Zach's head, stroking his hair. He looked just as he had after Bryce had fished him from the canyon pool. But now both of them were back in Milton, and it had happened again. He couldn't have come all this way only to lose his brother now. He'd never forgive himself.

"Please, God," he whispered in a desperate prayer, as Maggie and the others huddled with their hands clasped together.

When Zach didn't respond to CPR, the medic nodded to the other soldier who was waiting with a portable defibrillator machine. The medic stripped off Zach's wet shirt and placed pads connected to wires on his chest. "Clear!" he shouted, as the second man operated a small machine squealing with an electric charge. Zach's entire body bounced with the impact of the voltage.

Maggie gasped and turned her head. Andrew and Charlie grimaced, and Bryce steeled himself, determined to stay with his brother no matter the cost. It seemed cruel, after everything Zach had been through, to hit him with another jolt like that. Would it help, or was it draining him even more?

For a moment, Zach's body lay still. The medic nodded for the soldier to hit him with the charge again, but suddenly, Zach stirred. He coughed, a stream of water pouring from his mouth. The medic quickly turned him onto his side so he wouldn't choke.

A wave of relief flooded through Bryce's body as he watched his brother cough again and then fill his lungs with air.

"Zach, can you hear me?" the medic called.

Gradually, Zach's eyes inched open. He looked around.

"Zach!" Bryce cried, reaching back down and cradling his brother's head.

A collective sigh of joy filled the group around them as Zach looked up, his eyes slowly focusing. "Bryce? Is that really you?"

He grinned. "It's me, buddy. I'm right here." He wrapped his arms around Zach's shoulders and whispered in his ear. "You did it. You got me home."

* * *

AFTER ZACH SEEMED STABLE, Bryce moved back to give the medic room. He embraced Maggie, who clung to him like he was about to disappear again at any second. He broke free long enough to shake hands with Tyler and Professor Hendrickson. He slapped Andrew on the back, good-naturedly, and Andrew introduced him to Jess.

"Hey, you didn't forget about me, did you?" a voice

called behind him. Bryce spun around as Charlie pulled him into a huge bear hug.

"Dude!" Bryce exclaimed. "I'm so glad you aren't dead. This couldn't have happened without you."

Charlie laughed. "I told you when we met, man, it takes a lot from those fibberlickers to keep me down."

Bryce noticed that General Weber had pulled Professor Hendrickson to the side. They weren't arguing, but the discussion looked serious, and Hendrickson was mostly nodding at Weber's directions. When the general headed back to his men, who were already working to clean up the wreckage from the flood, Bryce and the rest of the group were eager for news.

"What's happening?" Zach called.

They all moved closer to where Zach was resting so he could hear. Andrew looked nervous. "Are we in trouble?"

"I wouldn't call it trouble." Professor Hendrickson flattened his lips. "Based on how all this ended, I think the general will get over whatever animosity he carried toward us."

Charlie exhaled. "So we're in the clear?"

"Listen," said Hendrickson. "You should all be very proud of what you accomplished during the past few days. Your bravery and support for each other is remarkable. The scientific breakthroughs we've achieved in the past few months, let alone the past few hours, are astonishing. They'd normally be recorded in publications and taught in universities around the world for years to come…"

"Uh-oh," said Bryce. "I sense a 'but' coming."

Hendrickson gave a weak smile. "The reality is that everything we've witnessed is extremely top secret. General Weber is uncompromising in his order that this all remain confidential until further notice."

Zach looked up. "You mean we *still* can't tell anyone?"

"What about our parents?" asked Jess.

Tyler put his hand on her shoulder. "He's right. There's too much uncertainty. We don't even know what's happened to Q2, to Yao and Fitz and their efforts to use the bridge."

Maggie looked at the hesitation on Hendrickson's face. "There's more, isn't there?"

The professor nodded. "Each of us will need to spend time in quarantine. After being in direct contact with the tremendous energy released from the bridge's transmission, it's safest for all of us to be fully evaluated."

Bryce motioned down to Zach. "What about us? We're the only ones who actually traveled across the bridge. Are they ever going to let us out?"

"The process will be more intense for you both, I'm afraid," Hendrickson acknowledged. "We know that something has happened to Zach since he encountered the virtual world. We'll hope that the dimensional disturbances from the bridge are over, but we don't know yet. He'll need to be monitored closely to ensure his symptoms subside. You'll need evaluation too, Bryce. You've been gone for a long time. We need to make sure your body hasn't developed symptoms like Zach's and that you aren't a danger to those around you."

Bryce closed his eyes. He knew Hendrickson and Weber

were right. They had to be sure everything was safe. But he didn't want to go away. He'd just come back.

Maggie squeezed his hand. "I can't lose you again."

Bryce draped his arm around her. "It's okay. It'll just be for a little while. It's the right thing."

General Weber walked closer and motioned to the professor that it was time to go. His men zipped the Ranger's body in a bright orange bag. The soldiers' shots had finally terminated the killer from the other world. He would likely be the subject of intense scientific probing, or perhaps be locked away deep within a secret government vault, maybe both.

Bryce looked back at Hendrickson. "Can I see my parents at least? I have to let them know that I'm back, that I'm safe."

"Me too," said Zach. "They've been through too much already."

The professor nodded tenderly. "I promise you we'll work something out. It may start in a secure environment, but you'll see them. I give you my word."

Bryce was suddenly weak. He pulled Maggie and Zach into a tight hug, grasping on to them for support. Tears streamed down his face. Everything was hitting him at once.

"Thank you."

CHAPTER THIRTY-FOUR_

The vortex of color was mesmerizing as Yao shot through time and space faster than the speed of light. His lungs pressed so tightly, he could barely breathe. The heat was almost unbearable, but he was used to enduring physical discomfort. The journey would be worth the pain when he reached his new dimension.

Finally, the pressure subsided. Everything went black, and he was floating through space.

He had done it. He'd crossed the bridge.

Far off in the distance, a speck of light appeared. It grew, slowly at first, and then with rapid acceleration. It was *his* kingdom. He was a god.

There was a burst of brilliant light, and then he was plunging through water. Yao opened his eyes as he tried to reverse the direction of his travel back up toward the surface. Millions of illuminated organisms floated all around him in beautiful synchronization. It was astounding.

Finally, his mouth cracked the surface. He wiped the water from his face and stared at his hands in anticipation.

He blinked his eyes. No! It couldn't be! Yao waved his withered, wrinkled fingers in front of him. Fitz had promised a new, youthful body, free of disease and age, that would carry Yao's essence for eternity. So what was this? His hands looked the same as before.

Yao gazed across the pool. He was in a cave, with a ceiling of rock high above him. It formed a perfectly curved dome that glowed in the water's light. But that was impossible. There was no design for such a space in his new world. Was this simply a stopping point along the bridge that Fitz had neglected to mention? What had Sturgis called out just before the beam had taken him?

Yao felt a current pulling him through the water. He peered at the far reaches of the pool and glimpsed a hint of movement. A lone fin rose above the surface. It sped toward him through the water.

Yao turned in a panic, willing his legs to kick, but he had no strength. A shooting pain filled the left side of his chest, like his heart had stopped beating.

His head slipped beneath the surface. He sank down into the bright water with his eyes staring wide. His body would not respond, and he could only watch in absolute terror as an enormous creature, like a serpent, surged toward him. Its jaws opened, revealing rows of glistening, razor-sharp teeth ready to devour him.

His mind, alert as always, instantly flashed through a

million questions, a million scenarios of what could have gone wrong. An answer came to him.

Yao's final thought was astonishment at how the young recruits had somehow gotten the better of him.

CHAPTER THIRTY-FIVE

L ife wasn't the same after Bryce came back across the bridge. At least not right away. Maybe it never would be.

Maggie, Andrew, Jess, Tyler, and even Professor Hendrickson had to spend a week in monitored quarantine at the Veterans Affairs hospital at Quantico where Zach had been held. Thankfully, the doctors kept everyone more informed this time, and they were all allowed to communicate with their families. There was nothing they could be told to satisfy their questions, but having their children back seemed to distract them from their anger. After that week, the others checked out fine medically and they were cleared to go home.

It took a while longer for the brothers. Bryce had demanded he be allowed to stay with Zach, and interviews and tests consumed most of their days. Team after team of scientists, doctors, high-ranking government officials, and who knows who else, walked through every detail of what they'd seen and done on the bridge and inside *Kingdom*. Their bodies were prodded, scanned, and measured in more ways than they'd ever thought possible. It was exhausting, but also extremely boring, and all they both wanted was to finally go home.

Hendrickson held to his promise, convincing General Weber to allow their parents to visit often. For the first few weeks, his mom and dad had to stay on the other side of a hermetically sealed glass panel for their own safety. It felt like they were visiting in prison. Bryce didn't complain, and it was wonderful to see his parents, but they all ached to hold each other in a long, tight embrace.

Maybe he and Zach really were dangerous, but Bryce didn't think so. He seemed to have escaped any noticeable physical ill effects from his travels. Zach's episodes gradually decreased and eventually disappeared completely. His hair grew back too, with only a small trace of white remaining.

Professor Hendrickson convinced General Weber that the boys' mom and dad deserved some explanation for what had happened to their sons. They didn't get the real story, or at least not all of it, but there were glimmers of truth in what his parents heard. Weber told them that Bryce was mistakenly pulled into a top-secret military exercise involving a deadly pathogen. With its potential to trigger a worldwide pandemic, the government had kept him locked away for his own safety and the safety of others. Zach had discovered the truth and, once he contacted his brother, had to be quarantined as well.

General Weber said he regretted not being more forth-coming earlier.

Bryce guessed the story made as much sense as anything else, if you didn't know better. It was hard to tell what was true anymore. So much in the world seemed like pure science fiction. If technology could transport people into the virtual world of a video game like *Kingdom*, there was no telling what could come next. But their parents didn't seem to question it. They were just glad to have their boys back home.

Even knowing what had really transpired, Bryce wasn't sure of the whole truth. They'd met with Hendrickson several times at the hospital. He told them that Weber and the rest of the government had finally agreed that a bridge to alternate dimensions was far too dangerous. The JOSHUA project was officially terminated. In fact, techni-cians were currently dismantling its machine in the cavern and the remains of the Eden machine in Q2's compound. Bryce guessed that the government would store the pieces somewhere deep within a top-secret facility, likely right next to the frozen body of the Sportsman.

No one in China could find any trace of Ji Yao. Appar-ently at the exact moment that Bryce had passed across the bridge, the top floors of Yao's skyscraper in Shanghai had exploded. Sturgis was reportedly killed in the accident, and Canadian Mounties had intercepted Fitz making a run for the northern border of Montana.

Fitz refused to talk without an immunity deal, but Bryce was certain the man had created a portal to the bridge over Yao's building in China. He didn't know if Yao had made it across, but it didn't matter. With the bridge and all of its systems permanently out of operation, Yao wasn't someone they needed to worry about.

* * *

WHEN THE GOVERNMENT finally released Bryce and Zach, summer was just around the corner. It had been nearly a year since their adventure had begun.

Bryce had missed his entire senior year, though he had taken a few online classes while in the hospital. Those, plus the extra credits from his AP classes, allowed him to still graduate on time. He and Maggie even made it to prom. It was all Bryce could do to fight back the tears when he walked across the stage at graduation and saw his mom and dad and Zach waving from the audience.

Rumors had been flying around the school all year about what had happened to him. Maggie said there were at least a dozen conspiracy theories—he'd been abducted by Somali pirates near Morocco, he'd worked on a lobster boat in Alaska, he'd been addicted to painkillers and was living under a bridge in New Jersey, or even that he'd been abducted by aliens.

If they only knew.

Some nights he would lie in his bed and dream about how different his life would have been if he'd never answered Q2's email. It almost didn't seem real. Sometimes he'd pretend he'd just dreamt it all. It was easier that way.

General Weber finally seemed to realize that Bryce was never on board with Yao and his devious plans. Maybe Weber just understood how badly their family had been screwed over. But either way, things improved when he relaxed his grip on their movement.

When Professor Hendrickson received a major government grant for one of his other fields of research, he hired Bryce's dad as head of communications and marketing. It meant the family would have to leave Milton to be closer to Tech. But they'd already had some offers on the house, and they all seemed ready for a change of scenery. Zach would miss hanging out with Andrew, but they could stay in touch online, and Zach was ready for a fresh start with high school in the fall. Bryce thought Andrew might have a thing for Jess Barnes, so he'd probably be fine without Zach around as much, too.

After the events at the water tower and his debriefings from within the VA hospital, Charlie had returned home to Edgarton to see his grandma and cousins. But Bryce didn't think Charlie would stick around there for long. He'd already mentioned taking a year off to travel out West. They'd promised to stay in touch, but Bryce doubted they'd ever see each other again. Too much had happened.

Bryce didn't know if Hendrickson had pulled any strings, but even having missed most of his senior year, he received a full-ride academic scholarship to Tech. He wasn't sure about track. He'd probably have to spend most of the summer building his strength back up. Coach Robb said he'd be happy to have Bryce try out as a walk-on, and Bryce figured he just might try it.

Tyler finished grad school and took a full-time position on Hendrickson's research team. He told Bryce that there was an internship and summer work waiting for him whenever he was ready. Some people, if anyone ever knew the whole story, might claim that the special treatment Bryce and his family received was unfair and that he'd brought all his troubles on himself through his actions. Maybe that was true. But they'd been through so much. Bryce thought they all deserved a second chance.

CHAPTER THIRTY-SIX_

Bryce pulled into Maggie's driveway and tapped the horn on his old Mustang. He felt almost like normal as he watched her skip down the porch steps.

Each time he saw her now, Bryce marveled at how beautiful she was, her kindness to others, and how lucky he was to still have her. Since she had been accepted by Tech's English department, they'd be together as freshmen in the fall. While he'd heard that most relationships from high school didn't last in college, he knew in his heart they were different.

Maggie slid into the passenger seat. She took his hand and stared into his eyes. "You're sure you don't mind me coming? It's okay… I'll understand if you need some space."

"No," he answered. "I want you with me."

"Are you sure?"

"Positive."

She squeezed his hand tightly, leaning in for a kiss. "I love you, Bryce."

He kissed her back and then tucked those words deep within his heart as he rolled down the windows and backed out of the driveway.

The green sign over the highway showed seventy miles to Limerick. Bryce had one more piece of the puzzle to complete. He had to help close the story for someone who would never go home.

Bryce had rehearsed a dozen times in his mind what he'd say when he knocked on Rachel's mom's door. He still wasn't sure what would come out when he opened his mouth, but he knew he had to tell her something. Rachel deserved at least that much.

Maybe there was no true explanation for what had happened. Who knows what worlds and possibilities lie outside our understanding of science and technology. But maybe we aren't supposed to know. Maybe some things are too perilous to explore. Perhaps it's enough to focus our attention right here—in our own dimension, time, and place.

Power and greed kept someone like Yao from being content with anything he could attain on earth. Flattery and pride almost cost Bryce everything—his family, his home, his life...

Bryce turned and watched Mags's hair blow loosely in the breeze. The way her smile etched across her face. The way she turned and looked at him.

And somehow, he just knew…

There was nothing left to find. Everything he needed was right there.

He was finally home.

ACKNOWLEDGMENTS_

Final Kingdom is the first series where I've made a conscious effort for a firm ending. Which is both exciting and a little sad. The books originated as a bit of a surprise after watching my then middle schoolers endlessly play *Fortnite*. *The Missing* sucked me in from the start, and I quickly knew there was a larger story to tell. It's been a fun time digging in a new sandbox—one for slightly older readers and with the open frontier of science fiction. I am not a science guy, so you probably noticed the wide berth I gave to the technical side. Hopefully the story sucked you in enough that you didn't question too many of the details behind the technology!

The first two books in the series were written in first person, *The Missing* was from Zach's perspective and *The Recruit* from Bryce's. I decided the best way to tell the wider story and wrap up the different loose ends was to write the conclusion in third person and alternate the chapters from different points of view. I wanted to tie things back to where they began, both with Zach, Andrew, Jess, and Maggie, but also with Bryce's fellow recruits Charlie and Rachel, the notorious crew over at Q2, and Hendrickson and Tyler. Writing the draft in the spring of 2020 during the COVID-19 pandemic pulled at the edges of the story and likely influenced a few of the scenes. The world is a much stranger place than when this story began, but I pray that you all stay safe and healthy, and that the wonder of reading provides a refreshing distraction during uncertain times.

As an independent publisher, I may be holding a lot of strings, but finishing a book as a group effort. Many thanks go out to my brilliant team, most of which have been with me on all or parts of my sixteen books—my editor, Kim Sheard, proofreader, Stephanie Parent, cover designer, Dane, and all my advance readers. Thanks to my family, particularly Mary and Aaron for being my first readers and edit on the entire series, and to Matthew, Josh, Mom and Dad, Haley, Gracie, and Lana for reading and supporting the series.

Finally, thank you to my readers. I hope the story captured your imagination as much as it did mine. See you on the next adventure!

Steven K. Smith is the author of *The Virginia Mysteries*, *Brother Wars,* and *Final Kingdom* series for middle grade readers. He lives with his wife, three sons, and a golden retriever in Richmond, Virginia.

For more information, visit:

www.stevenksmith.net

steve@myboys3.com

DID YOU ENJOY THE BRIDGE?_
WOULD YOU … REVIEW?

Online reviews are crucial for indie authors like me. They help bring credibility and make books more discoverable by new readers. No matter where you purchased your book, if you could take a few moments and give an honest review at one of the following websites, I'd be so grateful.

Amazon.com
BarnesandNoble.com
Goodreads.com

Thank you and thanks for reading!

Steve

Made in the USA
Las Vegas, NV
14 May 2024

89937456R00152